"Isabel's Different from Anyone I've Ever Known.

I feel like I'm sailing into uncharted waters."

There was an evil-sounding laugh. "And you love new territory, Mark. The harder she is to get, the harder you'll try. How long do you think it'll take?"

Mark laughed. "If I'm going to get her at all, I'm going to have to work fast. Her chances of making it in the department are slim to none."

Isabel moved from the door where she'd been eavesdropping. That conceited bag of wind! Lieutenant Mark Grady really did need a lesson in humility—and luckily for him, she was an excellent teacher.

AIMÉE MARTEL

lives in New Mexico with her teacher husband and three poodles. Writing romances, she says, is the only way that allows her to take the guilt out of her compulsive daydreaming.

Dear Reader:

SILHOUETTE DESIRE is an exciting new line of contemporary romances from Silhouette Books. During the past year, many Silhouette readers have written in telling us what other types of stories they'd like to read from Silhouette, and we've kept these comments and suggestions in mind in developing SILHOUETTE DESIRE.

DESIREs feature all of the elements you like to see in a romance, plus a more sensual, provocative story. So if you want to experience all the excitement, passion and joy of falling in love, then SILHOUETTE DESIRE is for you.

Karen Solem
Editor-in-Chief
Silhouette Books

AIMÉE MARTEL
The Fires Within

Silhouette Desire
Published by Silhouette Books New York
America's Publisher of Contemporary Romance

SILHOUETTE BOOKS, a Division of Simon & Schuster, Inc.
1230 Avenue of the Americas, New York, N.Y. 10020

ISBN: 0-671-47995-4

First Silhouette Books printing May, 1984

10 9 8 7 6 5 4 3 2 1

To Chief Sam Trujillo because he always took time to answer my questions, and never seemed to mind either the frequency or the number. But especially because when it was time for me to go into my deep, dark cave and write, he cared enough to get in touch and let me know that his help was only a telephone call away.

And to Bob Sullivan because he's been with me from the beginning and cares enough about my feelings to actually let me do the driving.

ACKNOWLEDGMENTS

With special thanks to Chief Leonard C. Ortega, Chief Ted Allred, Captain George Nichols, Fire Marshal Roy Gonzales, Sam Burnett, John Donato, Doc Harris, David Sisneros, David Gatley, and all the others from the Albuquerque (NM) Fire Department who gave me so much of their time.

To Tom Thurlo and the men of the Farmington (NM) Fire Department.

And to the men of the Rahway (NJ) Fire Department.

The Fires Within

1

Isabel strode up the concrete pathway leading to the substation. Taking several deep breaths, she tried to steady her jittery nerves. The temperature was a cool forty degrees, yet her hands were clammy and damp with perspiration; halting mid-step, she put down her worn duffel bag and rubbed them dry against her pants legs.

A cold gust of wind blew a strand of her copper-colored hair across her face. She tucked it back into her practical coiffure and paused for several seconds.

What was the matter with her? For the past few months she'd done little but look forward to her first day at work, and now she could scarcely build up enough courage to go inside. Being the first woman to graduate from the Academy should have prepared her for this moment. Cursing herself, she tried to brush her fears aside. It didn't work. There were just too many unanswered questions.

Would they look at her delicate features and fashion-model build and conclude she was just another pretty face, someone forced on them because of a law demanding a quota they violently opposed? The prospect filled her with dread. Her father had warned her she'd never be accepted. Her co-workers would view her as he did, someone who couldn't possibly do the job she'd been hired to do. She squared her shoulders. And that's where they were wrong. She could do the job, and she had every intention of doing so.

With a burst of determination, she approached the doors and walked inside.

A middle-aged man stationed by the radio console glanced up. His eyes traveled up and down her tall, willowy figure, appraising her thoroughly. "Can I help you?" he asked.

Isabel studied him. The large frame that had once supported muscle now had a tendency toward flab, and light reflected off the bald spot in the center of his head.

With a confidence she didn't feel, she unzipped her jacket and revealed her uniform and silver badge. She wanted to look implacable, professional to the core. Still, she didn't want to look too unfriendly. Hoping to convey with her emerald eyes what she couldn't put into words, she tried to soften her gaze. "I'm Firefighter Isabel Dailey. I'm to report to Lieutenant Grady. I begin night shift today."

"You're the new probie?" He seemed disturbed. "I think I read about you in the paper." His eyebrows furrowed; then he shrugged. "I'm Frank Lindsey, your friendly housewatchman."

She extended her hand. "Glad to meet you." Despite her smile, she was wary. The expression on his face was all too familiar. She'd seen it a thousand

times before. He was judging her by her sex, conclud-
ing that a woman of her slim proportions would never
have the stamina needed to cope with the hardships of
their profession. Yet, her looks were deceiving. In
reality, she was as strong as most men. Not that it had
come easily. It had taken months of grueling physical
workouts to build up her muscle tone. But it had paid
off. By the time she had arrived at the Academy, she'd
been able to compete with her male colleagues and
even best them on occasion. If there was one thing she
was determined to do, it was to prove to her father, as
well as all the other critics she had encountered, that
women firefighters could be every bit as good as the
men.

She answered his speculative glance with a disarming smile. "If you'll show me where I can find the
lieutenant, I'll get out of your way."

"He won't be back for another hour." The man
continued to watch her with the same curiosity one
might bestow on a particularly odd-looking insect.
"He told me we were expecting a new firefighter, but
he didn't tell me you were a lady. I'm not really sure
what I should do with you now."

Isabel smiled. "Why don't you show me my locker
and my bunk for starters?"

"I suppose," he said at length. He stood and
gestured for her to follow as he strode down the hall.

Isabel picked up her gear. Increasing her walking
speed to a semi-jog, she kept up with his quick pace.

As they traversed the apparatus room where the
pumper and rescue vehicle were parked, he glanced
behind him, checking to make sure she was still there.
Stopping by an open doorway, he waved her inside
with a casual sweep of his hand. "Your bunk is on the
far right."

The dorm consisted of approximately ten beds, she

estimated; tall metal lockers stacked against each concrete partition made it impossible to get an exact count. At least the dorm had been built with regard to an individual's need for privacy. That was a rare commodity at any station.

She dropped her bag on top of the bunk. "Thanks." Seeing no one around, she added, "Where is the rest of the company?"

"Watching TV in the rec room."

The look on his face clearly mirrored his misgivings. Isabel tried to put him at ease. "I guess I'm not exactly what you had anticipated."

He smiled back. "No, and I can assure you, you're going to come as quite a surprise to the loo."

Hearing a peculiar tone in his voice, she furrowed her eyebrows and met his gaze. "Meaning what?"

His lips pursed tightly. "Our platoon has been one man short for a while. Things have really been tough, particularly when we've had to work a fire." He shook his head. "We really need the extra help. So what do we get? A lady probie."

"You shouldn't assume that because I'm a woman I can't do the job," she replied gently. If she could keep her impatience from showing, and greet their objections with a little gentle persuasion, she'd have a much better chance of winning their respect. "If I hadn't been able to handle the work, I'd have never made it through the Academy. Remember, I had to pass the same tests you did."

He nodded slowly. "Well, we'll just have to see how you do around . . ."

He stopped in mid-sentence as the bells began to ring. "I've got to go." Jumping over the cot on his left, he landed in a sitting position by the edge of the mattress. In one fluid motion he kicked off his shoes, stepped into his boots, then pulled up the trousers

14

coiled around them. The process took only seconds, yet by the time he reached the door, Isabel had already donned her gear and was waiting for him.

"Where do you want me?" she asked quickly.

"Forget it," he yelled. "I'm not the loo. Wait for him." He ran to the garage, picked up his coat and helmet from a hook, then jumped onto the pumper.

Hesitating for only an instant, Isabel sprang forward. As the truck began to pull away, she leaped onto the back platform and held on. No way she was going to miss her first real working fire! Frank Lindsey, positioned on the other side, glanced at her in surprise, then turned away, suppressing a smile.

As the pumper wove its way through traffic, Isabel held on tightly. She still remembered the horror stories told during training about those who had lost their grip on the bar and had fallen to their deaths. Her heart began to race as she caught the scent of burning wood and plaster in the air. The fire was somewhere close by. As they turned the corner, she saw it. Smoke poured from the ground-floor window of a nursing-care complex.

The chief, already at the scene, seemed in the midst of a heated debate with one of the attendents. Isabel saw the woman gesture angrily toward the building as several patients were being wheeled out. The sign at the front read, "Good Samaritan, Home for the Aged."

As she adjusted her gloves, someone yelled to them, "We need five lengths of inch-and-a-half."

Frank Lindsey stepped off the back of the truck. Taking the nozzle in his left hand, he pulled his right through three folds of hose. As he stepped down, Isabel moved up and took another fifty-foot length. Dropping it on the ground, she reached for two more lengths of hose, then yelled to the driver, "Take off!"

The pumper moved to the hydrant as the coupled hose dropped off behind it.

Excitement, mingled with fear and apprehension, coursed through her. This was no practice run. Even though her thoughts were in a jumble, she somehow managed to remember what she was supposed to do. Placing two folds of hose over her shoulder, she followed Frank Lindsey inside the building. Her hands were trembling, but thankfully, everyone was too busy to notice. Luck seemed to be with her. It looked like she wouldn't even need an air mask this time around. She smiled to herself, glad she'd be spared the backbreaking task of having to carry an extra thirty pounds of equipment.

The hall was crowded with excited people. Isabel's eyes were glued on the civilians around her, warning them to watch the hose, when her foot caught on one of the lengths. Hurled forward, she smashed into Frank Lindsey's back.

He regained his balance with two steps, then turned and glared at her. "Will you watch what you're doing?"

She nodded miserably. "The hose disapproves of lady probies too and it leaped up and grabbed my ankle."

"If you think you can handle walking"—the curious half-smile on his face took the sting out of his words—"we better get back to work."

"Please!" She cringed slightly, wondering if perhaps she had just set the cause of women's lib back a hundred years.

"Let's go," he ordered.

The smoke began to thicken as they traveled farther inside the building. The fire was confined to an area at the end of the corridor, but the steam and heat rising from it escaped to all parts of the complex. Joining

16

firefighters from another station, they began battling the blaze.

"Where the hell have you guys been?" one of the men yelled.

Frank never took his eyes off the fire. "We stopped at the Four Seasons for dinner, you dumb-ass. What did you expect?"

Isabel started to laugh, but her attention was suddenly diverted when the hose began to vibrate in her hands. The line stretched and bulged as the nozzle in Frank's hand began to hiss air. Tightening her grip, she waited for the impact. Within seconds the hose came to life. The sudden burst threw her forward, but she managed to hold her ground. There was a chaotic explosion of sound as gallons of water, aimed inside the room, assaulted the ceiling. Large chunks of plaster began to fall, hissing and steaming, onto the wet floor.

Her flesh seemed to crawl in response to the hideous symphony echoing all around her. She was scared, but it wasn't the kind of fear that paralyzed. Instead, she felt exhilarated, proud of what she was doing despite the weariness seeping through her limbs as she continued to support the hose.

An eternity later—or so it seemed to her—the fire was out. Every muscle in her body ached as she helped the firefighters set up the Water Vak to siphon liquid from the flooded rooms.

The men working beside her had been strangers when the fire began, but now she felt a unique sort of camaraderie with them. She tried to read their expressions, wondering if they too felt the same way. It was impossible to tell.

Bending down to free part of a hose that needed to be coupled, she felt a dull ache at the back of her hand. Leaning against the wall, she looked down at her glove. A portion of it had been torn away and a long, narrow cut crisscrossed the back of her palm. Blood, flowing freely from it, trickled down her fingers. With a sigh, she edged out of the room and walked outside into the night air.

The rescue vehicle was parked alongside the pumper. She looked for the paramedics, but realized they were still inside assisting with the patients. Climbing onto the back of the van, she glanced around. A still figure lay shrouded by a red wool blanket. She did a quick double-take as she glimpsed the boots that protruded from beneath. So a firefighter had died. For several seconds she could do little else but stare. What had happened? Had he grown careless, or had his death been caused by circumstances beyond his control?

She tore her eyes from the lifeless body. Picking up some bandages from the supply box, she dressed her wound. Her injury suddenly seemed so inconsequential, she felt a twinge of guilt as she wrapped gauze around it.

Returning what was left of the roll to the box, she closed and fastened the lid.

"Loo?" a loud voice boomed over the radio.

Startled, Isabel jumped. Out of the corner of her eye she saw the shrouded figure begin to sit up. With a cry, she took a step back and toppled off the truck.

Tossing the blanket aside, he came toward her quickly. "Are you all right?"

"I thought you were . . . dead!" she blurted after a second's pause.

"Talk about a lousy first impression." He spoke a few hurried words into a hand-held radio, then focused his eyes back on her.

Still shaky from the encounter, she tried to hide her nervousness by launching an offensive. Brushing the

18

gravel from her pants with great flourish, she snapped, "Just what the heck did you think you were doing in there? If you're a firefighter, you should be fighting the fire."

She straightened up slowly and shifted her gaze to his face. His features were angular and sharply defined. The blue eyes seemed to have a crystal quality, much like translucent seawater. They shimmered, softly changing color under the harsh glare of the emergency lighting. Something about his bearing attested to his experience, both as a man and as a firefighter. He had about him that indefinable look of authority and assurance.

He gave her a very disturbing, knowing smile. "I don't owe you an explanation, but after that dive you just took, I'll give you one anyway." He cleared his throat. "I got an ember down my coat and it burned my back. One of our guys gave me a shot for the pain, but he either overestimated the pain or got me mixed up with an ox. It damn near put me out. I couldn't do much in there, so I came out here. I was freezing and wet, so I put the blanket over myself. I guess I must have passed out, because the next thing I remember is Artie yelling at me, and you flying out of the back of the truck."

Isabel sighed. "Well, I'm glad you're injured." She shook her head. "What I mean is, that it's an improvement over death." She covered her face with one hand. "This still isn't coming out right. Maybe I should hire a translator."

He laughed. "Don't worry about it." He leaned forward, trying unsuccessfully to find her name tag. "By the way, I'm Lieutenant Mark Grady." He flashed her a bright smile. "Who are you?"

She swallowed. Of all the people he could have turned out to be, why did it have to be *him?* "I was supposed to report to you, sir, but you weren't at the station when I arrived. I'm Firefighter Isabel Dailey."

"I'm sorry you didn't have a reception committee." His eyes mocked her. "I had a meeting with the chief. I was on my way back when the call came over the radio, so I decided to meet my crew here. I hope you approve."

"No, sir. I mean, yes, sir." She shut her eyes and shook her head. If only she could stop talking long enough to make some sense!

He laughed. "Welcome to Engine Company Fifty-five, Firefighter Dailey." He extended his hand.

As his fingers gripped hers, Isabel winced with pain.

Suddenly aware of the bandage, he pulled away immediately. "You better have the paramedics take a look at that."

"It's fine, sir."

"Have them look at it anyway." It was not a request. His tone left little doubt of that.

"Yes, sir." Even in his disheveled state, he was impressively handsome. Trying to keep her mind on business, she forced her eyes away from his and focused on his shoulders. It didn't help. Despite the loose jacket covering his body, he looked every inch the athlete. She glanced back at his face.

His expression mirrored a vague mixture of amusement and contempt. "So you're our new replacement."

"Yes, sir." She focused on his nose. At least there, he posed no distractions.

"Who told you to come on this run?" He pushed back several locks of brown hair that had fallen over his brow.

Here it came. She was in trouble already and she'd been on the job for only two hours. Perhaps she could brazen it out. "No one told me, sir. The alarm went off and I took a place at the rear of the pumper."

"You acted without waiting for orders, is that it?" His eyes narrowed. "Let me give you a warning, Firefighter Dailey. We don't condone rash behavior on the part of our firefighters, it can cause fatal accidents. From now on you don't act without specific orders; is that clear?"

"I thought I was showing initiative, sir." She realized how weak her explanation sounded the minute she heard herself speak.

"There's a thin line between initiative and stupidity, Firefighter Dailey."

She fought the lump at the back of her throat. Perhaps she had been a little too eager, but she certainly hadn't jeopardized anyone's safety with her actions. She knew her job. All she had wanted was a chance to prove herself. "You must have very little faith in the training the Fire Academy gives if you think my being here endangered any lives, Lieutenant. The way I see it, I lent a hand when one was needed."

His fists curled. It was obvious he wasn't used to being contradicted. "We'll talk about this back at the station, Dailey. Go back and finish whatever you were doing."

"Yes, sir."

Isabel could feel his eyes on her as she marched back into the building. She shouldn't have argued with him, even if she had thought she was being unjustly reprimanded. She exhaled loudly. Diplomacy just wasn't her forte. Mentally reviewing the encounter, she shivered. Between her inarticulate rambling and her inability to remain quiet when she should, she'd almost ended up torpedoing her own career before it even got started.

What had happened to her back there? Mark Grady was handsome, true, but that fact alone shouldn't have affected her the way it had. She was much too levelheaded. Stopping at the entrance, she turned and looked back at him. For better or worse, Mark Grady had awakened something in her, an awareness of her own femininity that was bound to make her life more difficult from now on. Muttering a curse, she strode inside.

Seeing the men engaged in a cleanup effort, and trying to decide where to start, she watched them for several seconds.

"Are you going to help, or do you plan on standing there?" Frank's voice broke through her thoughts.

She smiled as she began helping one of the men with the Water Vak. "I'm working, I'm working!"

By the time they returned to the station, Isabel's entire body was covered with a dense layer of soot and dirt. Her back ached and her arms felt stiff and sore. Too tired to even think, she moved automatically, scarcely aware of anything save the leaden feeling in her limbs. Silence hung heavily as she helped one of the firefighters stretch and hang the hoses to dry, while others readied fresh equipment for the next run.

After she'd finished, Isabel placed her coat and helmet on an empty hook near the pumpers, then dragged herself to the dormitory. With a reluctance born of weariness, she began to remove the rest of her firefighting gear. As soon as the men returned from the showers, she'd go to the bathroom, lock the door, and bathe. Clothed in a T-shirt and uniform pants, she sat on the edge of her cot and waited.

After forty-five minutes she walked to the bathroom and peered inside. It was empty. Locking herself in, she spread her things on a nearby bench, then stepped into the shower. The steaming water felt good against her skin. As the heat began to work its magic, she began to relax. Enjoying her first real break since reporting to work, she deliberately took her time. What she needed to do now was recoup her energy in case they had to respond to another alarm. That is, assuming the lieutenant would allow her to go with the other firefighters on the next run. Her status at the moment was uncertain at best.

Noticing a decrease in hot water, Isabel stepped out of the stall and dried herself off. Walking around the locker room in her underwear, she followed a familiar ritual. Picking up a bottle of lotion, she made herself comfortable on the wooden bench. Her skin felt shriveled after everything it had gone through. Pouring some of the thick white liquid into her palm, she rubbed it against herself vigorously. By the time she had finished dressing, she felt like a new person. Stopping in front of one of the small mirrors hung over the row of sinks, she brushed her hair until it shone, then tied it against the base of her neck with a strand of green yarn. Gathering her things, she unlocked the door.

As she pulled it open, she was confronted by an angry, soot-covered face. "What the hell have you been doing in there? I've been waiting for you to open this door for over an hour!" The lieutenant's voice was lowered to a growl.

Her heart raced as she stared at his ruggedly handsome features. Annoyed by her reaction to him, she tried a diversionary tactic. "I decided to take a bubble bath in the shower stall and had to wait for it to fill up." She smiled innocently.

He blinked. "Huh?"

Her eyes narrowed slightly as she grew determined to take control of the situation. After all, she was perfectly within her rights. The fact that he was handsome certainly didn't mean she was going to allow him to walk all over her. "What did you think I was doing in there, Lieutenant? I mean, for Pete's sake!"

The vein on his forehead bulged ominously. "What do you think this is? A college dorm? There are men in here, lady, that have as much right to that bathroom as you do—and that means *me!*"

"If you wanted to come in, you could have knocked."

"Kno . . ." He took a deep breath, then let it out slowly. "We have to have a talk. Come to the dining area in thirty minutes."

"Yes, sir."

She stood immobile as he strode past her into the locker room. Alone in the hallway, she exhaled loudly. She'd have to learn to get along with him, one way or another.

If only she had inherited some of her mother's passive temperament instead of her father's aggressive one. She shook her head slowly. No, she'd *never* be like her mother. If she had to take after someone, then she was glad to be like her Dad. It paid to be strong. The weak never achieved anything in this life.

Twenty-three minutes later, she walked to the kitchen. The station was quiet. Most of the men had either gone to sleep or were resting in their quarters. Glancing about and noting the lieutenant hadn't arrived, she walked to the cupboard, pulled out a jar of instant coffee, then filled a teakettle with water.

"Make enough for me too, okay?"

She turned her head. Wearing a pair of navy pants and an old flannel shirt he'd failed to button, Mark stood and met her long stare without flinching. "You know, you make me feel like a centerfold in a women's magazine."

Her face burned. She turned away, feeling as guilty as a kid caught with her hand in the cookie jar. "I don't know what you're talking about, sir." Trying to sound nonchalant, she added, "Do you take cream?" Her eyes were focused on his nose as she poured.

"First of all, I think you'll have better luck if you pour the water in the cups instead of on the counter." He gave her a slow, self-confident smile.

Isabel looked down. Suppressing the urge to swear, she yanked several paper towels from the dispenser and quickly began to wipe up the mess.

"Now, as to my second point, will you please stop staring at my nose? I realize that for some strange reason you feel uncomfortable looking me straight in the eye, but looking at my nose makes you go slightly cross-eyed."

Isabel closed her eyes and shook her head. Perhaps the Foreign Legion was accepting applications. "Lieutenant, do you think we can pretend I just walked in that door?" She gave him a sheepish smile.

He took a seat by the kitchen table. Chuckling, he rubbed his eyes.

She studied him carefully as she waited for his reply. The first thing that struck her was how weary he looked. Her eyes strayed to his lean, muscular chest. Wishing he'd button up his shirt and maybe grow a few warts, she took a seat on the other side of the table and forced her thoughts on business.

"Dailey, we're all going to have to do a lot of adapting around here." He gave her a wan smile. "I hope you realize that you'll have to compromise as much as anyone else. I might as well warn you right now, I won't tolerate you trying to take advantage of our good nature."

She pursed her lips tightly. "Would you care to clarify that?"

"You want clarification? I'll give you an example," he countered quickly. "Take this business of locking the door to the bathroom, then going into hibernation in there. That's got to go."

"I'm entitled to some privacy, Lieutenant!" If he thought he was going to browbeat her, he was in for one very big surprise.

"I can be reasonable, but my patience has limits." The curl at the edge of his lips could have passed for a smile if it hadn't been for the strain in his voice. "Fires have been discovered, fought and extinguished in the time it took you to take a shower."

Isabel stood abruptly. Resting her hands on the table, she leaned forward. "You're exaggerating just a little, don't you think?"

He faced her, giving her an unblinking stare, then pushed her gently back into her seat. "Sit down. We're not through yet."

The warmth of his palm penetrated through her workshirt. An aching awareness pulsed through her, momentarily displacing her anger and leaving her skin flushed with heat. Chiding herself for acting like a love-starved teenager, she sat.

For a few seconds he said nothing, then slowly he smiled. "If you'd been in that bathroom five more minutes, I'd have sent the paramedics after you. I thought you might have slid down the drain. Something like that would look terrible on my record. You had me worried."

Isabel blinked. "You're crazy." Suddenly she began to laugh.

He joined her. "Will you try to take less time in there from now on?"

"I give you my solemn word of honor."

"Now, I've got to tell you something you don't want to hear."

"Go ahead." There was no hostility in her tone.

He leaned back in his chair. "If you don't stop being so defensive about everything, you're not going to last very long at this job." There was a gentleness to his tone that precluded anger.

"You don't understand," she explained patiently. "There's a lot of guys in this department who can't stand the thought of a woman firefighter. I've had to deal with them by proving myself over and over again. If I'm as defensive as you say, then it's a reflex action."

He nodded. "Just remember that your probationary period is a time for learning. You're going to make mistakes and be reprimanded for them. Accept it."

"You're right." Isabel shifted uncomfortably, then averted her gaze. A warning echoed somewhere in the back of her mind. Mark Grady could be a dangerous enemy but an even more dangerous friend.

Standing, he yawned and stretched. "I'm beat. Let's go hit the sack."

She nodded, following him to the door.

2

The wake-up alarm sounded at seven with one short blast. Isabel rubbed her eyes. She hadn't slept much. Her attraction to Mark Grady was beginning to worry her. Tossing the covers aside, she lay still, staring at the ceiling.

Under ordinary circumstances she'd have gone to great lengths to avoid a man like Mark. His air of subtle arrogance attracted her, but it also reminded her of her father.

Being the fire chief's daughter had never been easy, but she realized it had been much worse for her mother. Isabel had seen the fear in her mother's face every time her father was out working a fire, as well as the relief when he returned home. Yet, even though Isabel loved and idolized her father, she'd never been blind to the fact that he'd made a less-than-perfect husband. He had demanded much of her mother, yet had given little in return.

Although he'd expected his wife to remain at home, he had always put his career first. In time, her mother became an extension of him, seeming to lose her own identity in her eagerness to adjust to his.

Isabel had watched, swearing that she would never allow that to happen to her. She'd keep a firm grip on her life, and never relinquish that control to anyone else. When she married, it would have to be to a man whom she could control, rather than one who might control her. Her attraction for Mark threatened the foundation of the promise she had made to herself years ago. He had a way of sweeping past her defenses, leaving her confused and vulnerable.

Now for the first time in her life she could see herself going down the same path her mother had chosen. There had to be a way to deal with the problem effectively. Perhaps what she needed was time to get to know him a little better—familiarity might breed contempt. With constant exposure, before long she'd be able to laugh about her infatuation and wonder what she'd ever seen in him.

Muffled voices echoed through the wall, disturbing the silence around her. A quick glance around the partition confirmed that she was the only one still in bed. Dressing, she walked to the bathroom. The last sink on the right was empty. As she strolled in, one of the men looked up and took a slice off his chin with a razor. "Lady, where do you think you're going?"

"Cool it, Dennis." She recognized Frank Lindsey's voice. The rest of the men were still a mystery to her. Everyone, including her, had been too tired for introductions the night before.

One of the firefighters turned his back to her, quickly adjusting his pants.

Isabel walked to the sink, plugged her curling iron into a nearby outlet, then loosened the rubber band that held her long hair in a ponytail. A slow transformation took place as Firefighter Dailey gave way to Isabel Dailey, the woman. As she dabbed a final touch of makeup on her face, she faced the astonished men around her and gave them a wide smile. Not waiting for a response, she walked out the door and headed for the kitchen. Pouring herself a cup of freshly brewed coffee, she waited as the men began trickling in.

Mark Grady came into the room, grinned and gave her a playful wink. She started to return the gesture but stopped, annoyed by his presumptuousness.

As Mark began the introductions, she stepped forward, shaking hands with each of the four men. First there was Artie Milanaro, a dark-haired, olive-skinned man who looked as if he had been built by the same firm who had constructed the stone giants at Easter Island. Next came Dennis Kerry, a red-haired Irishman who looked at her with the same distaste one might reserve for something that had crawled out of the woodwork. The third in line was Frank Lindsey. She greeted him with warmth, acknowledging their previous meeting. Joe Gutierrez was the last. Shorter than the others, he had thick curly black hair and brown eyes. Nothing about him seemed noteworthy except his smile, which suggested an enormous zest for life.

As they waited for the day shift to arrive, they sat around the kitchen table sipping their coffee.

"What makes a pretty woman like you want to go out and do a man's job? Particularly one as dirty as ours?" Joe baited.

"It's the rubber clothes that turn me on," Isabel retorted matter-of-factly.

The coffee cup slipped out of Joe's grip, spilling the steaming liquid all over Mark's hand. Jumping up,

Mark ran to the sink and put his hand under cold water.

While Joe kept Mark busy with apologies, Isabel walked to the refrigerator, took out a handful of ice cubes, then wrapped them loosely in a paper towel. Traversing the kitchen, she approached Mark. "Give me your hand."

He eyed her with suspicion. "What for?"

She gave him a blank stare. "Because you're so devastatingly handsome that I can't resist the urge to hold your hand."

Giving her a dirty look, he complied with her request.

His palm felt rough and masculine against hers. Forcing herself to maintain a pose of clinical detachment, she supported his hand while placing the makeshift ice pack on the injured area.

The men watched Mark carefully. His eyes, in turn, were glued on Isabel. "Most women appreciate the fact that I'm hot-blooded, but even if it fails to impress *you*, don't you think this is a ridiculous way to cool me off?"

The men howled.

"No." Isabel smiled, then muttered softly, "Ridiculous is the dance you're going to do if I decide to drop this down your pants."

Hearing her, he began to reply, but stopped as their replacements began to come in.

Isabel grabbed Mark's free hand and placed it over the ice pack. "You're on your own."

Accepting the curious stares aimed in her direction, she returned to the dorm, picked up her purse, then walked outside into the crisp morning air. There was a slight breeze, but her white turtleneck sweater offered ample protection against the cold. Enjoying the beautiful morning, she strolled to the bus stop. She didn't even mind taking the bus until she could afford to pick up her car from the shop where it was being repaired.

She had just arrived at the corner when a dark blue sedan pulled up beside her. "Isábel, do you need a ride?"

She turned around. Mark Grady's smile was contagious. Despite the temptation to accept his offer—or perhaps because of it—she shook her head. "No, thanks. The bus should be here in a couple of minutes."

"Aw, come on! My company beats that of the bus driver any day." Pulling up to the curb, he walked to the passenger's side and held the door open. "If you don't accept my offer, you're going to make me look really stupid."

She didn't have to look to know everyone around the bus stop was staring, waiting for her reaction. Hating him for putting her in such an awkward situation, she stepped into his car. As she slid in, she began having second thoughts. "Lieutenant, this really isn't—"

"We're off duty, now, so why don't you call me Mark?" There was a practiced smoothness in his tone. Instinct told her Mark Grady was a man used to having his own way, particularly when it came to women. "You're not scared of me, are you?"

Turning her head, she looked directly at him. "We're off duty, right?"

"Of course. Anything that happens between us now is strictly off the record." He gave her a teasing look.

The conceit of the man! Did he really expect her to fall at his feet and die of gratitude because he had deigned to flirt with her? "First of all"—she struggled to keep her voice even—"I assure you I'm not in the slightest bit afraid of you."

He interrupted her before she had a chance to complete her thought. "Then why are you acting so skittish?"

"Acting so . . . Lieutenant—"

"Mark," he interrupted again.

She closed her eyes and took several deep breaths. "Now you're angry."

"How remarkably perceptive of you!"

Mark stopped at the next intersection. "Where to?"

"Nowhere, with you." Taking advantage of the red light, she began to open the door.

Reaching over, he placed his hand over hers. "Wait, please."

She didn't know why, but she did as he asked. "I'm waiting."

"Don't be angry. I just wanted to be friends. Can't we work together and be friends too?"

"I don't know."

The candor in her voice made him laugh. "Well, that's certainly telling me."

She laughed too. "Look, Mark, I'm going to have enough problems during my probationary period. I don't want to be at odds with my lieutenant too. I'm not saying we can't be friends, but I want you to think of me as one of the guys, okay?"

"Don't you like being a woman?"

She knew he was deliberately goading her; still, she had no intention of backing down. Bracing herself for a confrontation, she stared at him. "That was a cheap shot."

"Maybe, but on the face of what you just said, it's an honest question."

"I like being a woman, but when I'm on the job or when I'm dealing with my co-workers, I'd rather be thought of as just another firefighter. I want to succeed at this job, and believe me, being female isn't a plus."

"Why do you think becoming a good firefighter means you can't be treated as a lady?"

"It simply doesn't work. From what I've seen, the men will only accept me as an equal if we're all on the same footing. When we're out on the line, they have to think of me as another trained professional. I don't want them to feel protective because of my sex and I don't want any special consideration. That can get them killed." She paused. "Can you understand that?"

"Very well."

"Now, tell me why you were needling me." Being around this man was like dropping matches on herself and seeing how long it took her to catch on fire.

"I'll answer that if you'll tell me where you live. I don't want to drive around this block one more time, if I can help it."

Isabel laughed. "All right. I'm at 474 Palm Acre Drive."

He looked at her quickly. "You're kidding."

"No, why should I be?" She paused. "Unless you know something about the building that I don't know. Don't tell me it's been condemned or something."

He laughed. "No, but guess what? We're neighbors! I live at the Bal Harbour Apartments, across the street from you."

"You're kidding." Isabel smiled, but her mind was busy weighing the implications of what she had just learned. The apartments across the street were known as a swinging-singles place. Six months ago, during her search for a place to live, she'd looked them over but had decided against moving in. Any place dubbed a haven for swingers was certainly not for her.

The fact that Mark, on the other hand, had chosen to live there told her a great deal about him. It figured that on top of all the other drawbacks she could think of, he was also the type who liked to add periodic notches to his bedpost. Well, if he intended on making her his next conquest, he was certainly heading for trouble. She had no intention of becoming any man's temporary distraction.

She looked at him for a second, then glanced out the window. Perhaps this was her lucky day after all. Hadn't she hoped to find something that would kill the attraction she felt for him? This certainly qualified.

Unexpectedly she began to have doubts. Perhaps she was jumping to conclusions. She pondered the question. Well, there was only one thing to do. She'd sit back and watch. If he was the kind of man she suspected him of being, he'd soon show his true colors. Then and only then would she feel justified in turning the tables on him and giving him an object lesson in humility.

Reaching over, Mark placed his hand over hers. "Don't be so uptight around me. I promise I'm not the big bad wolf."

"I'll keep it in mind, if you remember I'm not Little Red Riding Hood." As his fingers entwined around hers, Isabel's pulse began to race.

He laughed. Parking in front of her building, he left the car and held the door open for her. "I have a couple of errands to run this morning, but how about joining me at my place for lunch?"

She hesitated, clearly tempted by the offer. "I don't know . . ." Maybe it was safer to give him a wide berth.

"What are you worried about?"

"You." She smiled. "Why are you being so good to me?"

"Because I happen to think you're beautiful, bright

and very dedicated." He smiled back. "And because there's a certain openness about you I find very appealing."

"The qualities you've just described could also apply to a cocker spaniel."

"I find you more appealing."

"That sounds like a compliment. Why doesn't it feel like a compliment?"

He laughed. "So how about lunch?"

"Mark, I don't even know you yet . . ."

"Look at this as your golden opportunity."

She had meant to say no, but instead she heard herself saying something quite different. "All right. How can I pass up the chance for indigestion in the company of such a handsome man?"

"Indigestion? I'm a great cook! I promise I'll dazzle you with my skills!"

"Well, don't worry. If part of that treat includes ptomaine, I have real good connections in the fire department. We'll be able to get the paramedics over in record time." She smiled. Keep joking, Isabel, she told herself grimly. Maybe you can salvage something out of the mess you've just created.

Wearing a pair of her favorite designer jeans and a bright green V-neck sweater, Isabel scrutinized her appearance in the mirror. Her jade-colored eyes sparkled with excitement; her shoulder-length copper hair shone brightly in the light. She was grateful that the department had let her keep it long, though she had to be able to keep it tucked under her helmet. Brushing the bangs away from her eyes, she continued to stare at her reflection. Did she look all right? She wanted to look nice, but not so nice as to make Mark believe she'd actually gone to any extra effort. With a shrug she rechecked the time. She was supposed to be at

Mark's in another five minutes. Walking to the front door, she stepped outside.

The temperature was chillier than usual for late April in the Rockies. Living in the small city of Brighton, Colorado, however, had definite advantages. Although winters were often extremely snowy, the summers were cooler than in any of the neighboring states. For an avid fan of the outdoors like she was, Brighton was the perfect place to live.

A gentle breeze rustled through her hair as she walked across the parking lot outside Mark's apartment building. The closer she got to his apartment, the more her throat tightened with anticipation. Why hadn't she refused his invitation? She quickened her pace and tried to exercise her apprehension away. It didn't work. By the time she arrived at his door, her palms were clammy. Taking a deep breath, she rapped lightly on his door.

He answered almost immediately. His eyes traveled up and down her frame appreciatively. "Wow! You look great."

Imitating his appraising look, she smiled. "Thank you." Why couldn't Mark have at least one feature that was unappealing? Determined to find something that she could zero in on, she narrowed her eyes thoughtfully and resolved to search harder.

He stepped aside, allowing her to enter. "What? You're not going to return the compliment? Surely you were able to find at least one thing you liked."

Realizing he had misconstrued her look, she smiled with satisfaction. "I wasn't looking at you. I was just checking your ceiling tiles and your carpet."

"Uh-huh. And if I believe that, you're more than eager to show me a bridge I might be interested in, right?"

Seeing the mischievous twinkle in the blue eyes, she

began to laugh. "But it's going for such a good price! How can you resist such a fantastic business deal?"

"What can I say? I'm a cynic. It must have something to do with that land I bought in Florida—while the tide was out." Walking to a bar in the far corner of his living room, he pulled out a bottle of wine. "It's my finest. Want a glass?"

"What kind is it?"

He picked up the bottle and made a show of holding it up to the light. "Red," he said at length.

"I can't tell you how wonderful it makes me feel to know the care you took to find the right vintage," she added with a laugh. Despite her efforts to the contrary, she found herself liking him more and more. His lack of pretentiousness charmed her. He was so easygoing and confident—so much like her father. The thought stopped her cold, sending a shiver up her spine. No! She would not make the mistake of allowing her emotions to take over. She was determined to prove to herself that she could handle any man, including one as appealing as Mark.

"Only the best for such a beautiful lady." Mark handed her a glass. Their eyes met for only a second, but Isabel felt sure he had read her thoughts. She shifted nervously and averted her gaze. "Now I better check the hamburgers," he said. "I'm barbecuing outside on my porch."

"Let me help." She started toward him, eager for a chance to get busy, but he stopped her.

"There's really not much for you to do, so why don't you relax and make yourself at home?"

"Does that mean I can look around without a native guide?" Maybe that would be a good way of finding out more about him, without getting too personal.

"Certainly. Be nosy! Blast convention!"

She made a face. "Go ahead and be hostile. I'll charm you in the end, anyway."

He stopped by the sliding glass door and turned around. "You've already charmed me. I'm yours anytime you want."

Her heart leaped to her throat. Wishing she'd never said anything, she gave him what she hoped looked like a confident smile. "Right," she added nervously. "Next solar eclipse, I'll give you a call."

As he stepped outside, Isabel heard a scuffling noise that made her hair stand on end. She turned around quickly. It had come from the study. Cautiously she peered inside the room. Nothing seemed amiss. Her flesh crawled as she recalled the sound. Only one thing could make a noise like that. With a burst of courage, she decided to take a closer look. Surely she was mistaken. There couldn't be any rodents in an expensive complex like this one! After making a visual check through enough to satisfy her conscience, she decided to join Mark on the balcony.

She had reached the doorway when she heard it again. As she turned, she caught a glimpse of something large and furry darting behind a file cabinet.

"Mark, I think you better get in here." She stood by the doorway, shaking her head in disgust. Rats didn't scare her, but they did make her nauseous. Some people had the same reaction to roaches, others to snakes. For her it was rats. There was just something about them that made her flesh crawl.

He was at her side in an instant. "What's wrong?"

"I don't know how to tell you this, but you have rats in this place."

His puzzled look vanished as he began to laugh. "I think you've just had the pleasure of meeting one of my pets."

She suppressed the shiver she felt running up her spine. "You keep rats as pets?"

He shook his head. "They're not rats. They're ferrets." He traversed the room and reached behind the file cabinet. "Okay, guys. Fun's over. Come out and meet our guest."

The wriggling mass of fur squeaked in protest as Mark pulled it out of its hiding place. "This is Odysseus, or Ody for short."

He held it out to her. Realizing it was an obvious signal for her to take the little animal from him, she gave him a wan smile.

"Go on. They're harmless."

Grasping it firmly in her hands, she held it against her. "Hello, Ody."

"Watch your nose. They like to nip."

Instantly she pulled it away from her. "Wonderful. What else do they like to do?"

He laughed, then pulled another one, a smaller version of the first, from behind the closet. "Here you are." He walked toward her. "This is Penny. She's not quite as good-natured as the boy, but then again, females seldom are."

"I hope you're referring exclusively to ferrets."

He grinned. "Actually, I think it holds true for all females, regardless of species."

"You do, do you?" She looked at him sardonically. "Well, it doesn't matter. I'm not here because I'm impressed with your reasoning powers. As far as I'm concerned, you're just another pretty face."

"Ouch! Are you saying you don't think I'm very bright?"

She gave him a teasing smile. "No, but what's my opinion against thousands of others?"

Sitting on the floor, she began to play with Ody.

The ferret, in turn, seemed determined to steal her shoe. Laughing, she rolled him on his back and scratched his stomach. "They're adorable. Tell me one thing, though. Where did you get their names? I think, if anything, I expected something like Fred and Wilma."

"Odysseus and Penelope were characters in Homer's *Odyssey.*"

"I remember—Penelope was the ever-faithful wife, and Odysseus the adventurer."

"That's right."

"You're full of surprises. I mean, those aren't the kind of names that roll off your tongue."

"What do you expect from someone with a master's in English literature?"

"Why in the world would you spend that many years studying English just to become a firefighter?"

"Now, there's tact for you!" He laughed. "My family insisted that I get a degree, so I went to college to appease them. After I got my master's, then I went out and did what I wanted to do all along."

As the ferret scurried away, Isabel sniffed the air cautiously. "Something's burning."

"The hamburgers!" He shot out of the room. Isabel followed inches behind.

As he stared at the four circular pieces of charred meat over the grill, he muttered a loud curse. "So much for these." He slid each one onto a spatula, then dropped them into the garbage.

"It really doesn't matter," Isabel said softly. "We'll just have chips and wine for lunch."

He shook his head. "I don't know about you, but I'm starved. What do you say we get a couple of lunch boxes at the fried-chicken place down the street?"

"I'll get my purse."

"I have a better idea. You can stay here and listen to my records while I do the legwork. It's only fair, since I messed up lunch."

Isabel smiled. "It's okay with me. I'll baby-sit the ferrets while you go out in search of food. Sounds rather basic, too, don't you think? Like the caveman of old and his mate?"

He opened the door, then glanced back. "Hold that thought about the mate. I'll be back in less than five minutes."

As the door clicked shut, Isabel walked to his record collection and began to look through it. He was into jazz. She hated it. It sounded to her like a gathering of musicians each playing a different tune that miraculously ended at the same time.

Hearing the sound of laughter, she opened the front door. Leaning over the railing, she watched as several couples began playing a game of volleyball in the courtyard. Suddenly she heard a scurrying sound behind her; a ferret had escaped and was dashing down the corridor at an alarming speed.

Closing the door so the other one couldn't get out, Isabel chased after it. She managed to corner Ody as he reached the end of the hall. Trying not to scare him, she squatted down on all fours and began to extend her hands slowly. Suddenly the door to the stairwell flew open, hitting her resoundingly on the buttocks. She toppled forward, but still managed to catch the animal firmly in her grasp.

"Gawd, I'm sorry!" A chubby young man stared at her backside, then moved his gaze to her face. "What are you doing?"

Picking herself off the floor, she smiled sheepishly. "Trying to catch this." She held the ferret in front of her.

"Mark's ferret!"

"I let it out by mistake." She brought the creature close to her and stroked its sleek fur. "If you'll excuse me, I'll take him back now."

Hoping against hope he wouldn't tell Mark, she returned to the apartment. Putting Ody down, she watched him scamper away, taking a rubber toy with him. Of all the luck! It was bad enough to have let the ferret out, but to run into one of Mark's friends . . .

Hearing footsteps at the end of the hall, she walked to the door and peered out. Mark was exchanging a few words with his friend. If that man squealed on her, she wanted to know about it, so she strained forward to listen, taking care to remain out of sight.

"That's some lady you got this time, pal," the man was saying. "What happened to Linda?"

"I had to stop seeing her. It got to a point where the only thing she could talk about was marriage. I tried to tell her it wasn't something I was interested in, but she didn't listen."

"I should have it so rough! By the way, where did you find this one?"

"She's a new firefighter at my station."

"That figure of hers is enough to make me want to join the department!" He paused. "Wait a minute. I thought you told me you hated the thought of women firefighters. Did you change your mind?"

"No way. But if we're going to be stuck with them, I hope they all turn out to be as gorgeous as Isabel."

"Forget it. You just got lucky."

"Let's hope my luck's just beginning. Isabel's different from anyone I've ever known. I feel like I'm sailing into uncharted waters."

There was an evil-sounding laugh. "And you love

new territory. Let's face it. You were never able to resist a challenge, Mark. The harder she is to get, the harder you'll try. Poor thing doesn't have a chance. How long do you give her before you have her eating out of your hand?"

Mark laughed. "If I'm going to get her at all, I'm going to have to work fast. I doubt if she'll be around that much longer. Her chances of making it in the department are slim to none."

Isabel returned to the couch. That conceited bag of wind! She'd been right about him all along. Lieutenant Mark Grady really did need a lesson in humility. And lucky for him, he was going to have an excellent teacher.

Hearing him approach, she walked to his records and pretended to browse. "Hi there, that certainly didn't take you long."

"It's just around the corner."

They ate their lunch at a leisurely pace. When they had finished, Isabel helped him clear the table. As she stood by the sink, he came up from behind and placed his arms around her waist. His lips brushed the base of her neck.

Her body tensed as he touched her.

"Come on. Let's go sit down and talk."

She allowed him to lead her to the couch. Her mind raced as she tried to stay two steps ahead of him. Obviously he was about to make his move. Weighing her options, she decided to play along. She'd allow him certain liberties, then pull the rug out from under him. If anyone was going to fall head over heels, it wouldn't be her—she was more than a match for a man like Mark Grady.

With a casual air he placed his arm around the back of the couch, then allowed his palm to brush her shoulder. Instead of the cool composure she'd hoped to retain, she began to feel trapped. Silence grew between them. In the small room, it was impossible to ignore his masculine aura. Every nerve in her body seemed acutely aware of him. There was a physical presence about him, a kind of sensual appeal in his body and the way he moved that few men possessed.

Angry at herself for weakening, she shifted in her seat, then faced him. "So tell me a bit about yourself."

Isabel shivered as he began toying with a strand of her hair. Forcing herself to act as if she were scarcely aware of him, she tried to block out the sensations his touch created.

"You have such beautiful hair," he said in a husky voice.

Looking away, she cursed herself for being dumb enough to actually want to believe his line. "I've seen my hair. I see it every time I look in the mirror. That's old stuff to me. Tell me something about yourself."

He seemed intent on ignoring her. "It's such a beautiful color. It reminds me of burning embers."

Again with the hair. She moved slightly away, hoping to stop the tide of emotions his touch left in its wake. "Why don't we use this time to try to get to know each other? For instance, besides firefighting, do we have anything else in common?"

He gave her a slow lazy grin. "We're of the same species, and we live in the same hemisphere."

"How cozy. Just you and me and three hundred million other people."

He moved closer to her. "Why are you so nervous?"

"Nervous?" She tried to sound detached, but her voice broke. "I'm not the least bit nervous."

His hand slipped beneath the mass of russet hair and toyed with the skin at the base of her neck.

Isabel shuddered. She had to find a way to regain

the advantage. She was not one of those helpless females who crumbled under a man's touch . . . or was she?

No, of course she wasn't! She answered her own silent question firmly. Mark certainly wasn't her type. Overbearing playboys never had been. . . .So what harm could there be in enjoying a kiss or two?

Before she had completed the thought, his mouth was over hers. His tongue, intent on its prize, gently parted the soft lips beneath his.

A voice inside warned her to push him away, but her body turned liquid, consumed by the passion he was igniting within her.

"Isabel, don't be afraid of what's happening between us," he murmured against the softness of her neck.

All reasons for stopping were quickly whirling out of her reach. She shivered as her defenses began to crumble under the onslaught.

His hands caressed her throat as his lips moved downward sensitizing her skin. The gentle mastery of his love play enticed her deeper and deeper into his web. Her hands clutched at his shoulders, digging into the hard muscles.

Shifting, he pushed her backward onto the couch. Isabel tried to protest, but the words were caught in her throat. Using his strength to crush her resistance, he positioned himself above her, then slid his hips between the cradle of her thighs.

Her heart drummed in her ears as she tried to resist the unbearable, burning ache at the pit of her stomach. It had been crazy to think she could outwit him at his own game. As his hand slid beneath her sweater, Isabel heard herself moan. The weight of his body pressed her down, restraining her as he boldly slid her sweater out of his way and looked down at her exposed curves with unabashed wonder. "You're so beautiful, so incredibly tempting."

Her eyes widened as he lowered his mouth to her breast, one hand pushing aside the lacy material of her bra. Moistening the rosy-brown center, he rolled his tongue around it, then nibbled at it gently. Isabel cried out at the intensity of her reaction. Rational thought had fled, and all that remained was sensation.

"Easy, sweet," he whispered, his voice raw with desire.

Instinctively her arms encircled him, pulling him against her as her body arched to meet his. Curving one hand around his neck, she brought his lips toward hers once more.

His ravaging kiss left her gasping for air. His tongue penetrated the hidden recesses of her mouth, mating with hers in a ritual courtship of desire.

"I want you," he murmured.

The words brought reality crashing down on her. She couldn't give in to this man. They meant nothing to each other—or rather she represented a challenge to him, and he . . . Isabel shook her head, trying to clear it. She wasn't going to think about what he might mean to her.

There was a wild desperation to her voice as she pushed him away and said, "Please! Don't do this. It isn't right between us."

Something in her tone made him stop. "Isn't right? Admit it, Isabel. You want me right now just as badly as I want you."

"I can't think this close to you," she said, slipping out from under him.

Isabel stood and straightened her clothes. With a great deal of effort, she turned around and faced him. As she looked at him, she fought an overpowering sense of regret. She glanced away for a second, then focused back on him. "I'm not the kind of person who enjoys games, Mark. I won't play at love. It means too much to me."

"You want me, Isabel. Why are you fighting yourself?"

Her throat felt dry. "I have to. I won't demean myself by allowing you to turn me into another conquest. Your attitude cheapens me as well as you. I have no intention of settling for a crude imitation of the tenderness and depth of feeling a man and a woman about to make love share. I'm worth more than that, and by God I deserve better!"

She picked up her purse from the chair and slung it over her shoulder.

"What have you heard about me?" he asked, his voice surprisingly harsh.

"Enough to know that you enjoy playing very dangerous games. You and I are going to have to work together for the next few months. It's not going to help either one of us if we end up hating each other. I don't want to turn you into an enemy, but I can't give you what you want."

"Being enemies is not what I had in mind."

She took several steps to the door. "I know what you have in mind, Mark. What I'm trying to say is, it won't work. Find yourself another playmate."

As his telephone began to ring, he grabbed her hand. "Wait."

The second he picked up the receiver, she turned and walked out of his apartment.

3

Isabel stopped by the bulletin board. The work roster had just been tacked up. Checking her duties for the week, she groaned loudly. She had been elected to mop the floors and do the dishes. For this she had refused to follow the more traditional path and become a housewife?

Artie Milanaro gave her a sympathetic pat on the shoulder. "It's all part of being a probie, kiddo. You'll get all the dirty jobs until you get seniority."

"That's *if* she ever gets it," Dennis Kerry added.

Isabel gave him an icy stare. "I'll make it, mister. Don't you worry about that."

Dennis shrugged. "Whatever you say."

As he walked away, Artie gave her an apologetic smile. "Don't worry about him. He'll come around after he gets used to you."

"I'm not so sure." She pursed her lips as she

watched him walk down the corridor. "His type is stubborn to the end."

"Trust me. He's not bad at all, just a bit on the traditional side."

Isabel glanced at her companion. Artie was built like a wedge. Every inch of him seemed solid muscle. "And what about you? What do you think?"

"If you want it badly enough, you'll make it." He met her gaze. "What beats me is why you'd want it at all. It couldn't be the pay."

She joined his laughter. "Where else could I find a job that would allow me to live in relative discomfort for the rest of my days?"

Joe Gutierrez came up and peered at the board. "Thank God we have a probie! Now I know I won't get the dirty work."

"Thanks," she replied acerbically.

He gave her an appraising glance. "I've been trying to figure you out, and I think I finally have a handle on you." His eyes sparkled.

She smiled at him. "Care to share that piece of insight with me?"

He smiled back. "Are you any relation to Bob Dailey?"

"The former chief?" Artie's voice rose incredulously.

Isabel remained silent for a few seconds. She had hoped to keep her identity a secret but there was no escaping it now. "He's my dad. That's one of the reasons I became a firefighter."

"Our ex-chief's your dad?" Artie's eyes were wary.

She recognized the tone and the look. No matter what she did or said, the men would believe that there was only one reason why she was here: interoffice politics. Isabel exhaled slowly. Without another word, she walked to the kitchen. From this point on she'd have to fight a tough battle. The men would never accept her now, not until she proved herself.

Wondering how long it would take before the news reached Mark, she pulled a bucket from the janitorial closet and walked to the sink.

When Isabel had finished the floors, she walked out into the hall. Stopping mid-stride, she tried to decide whether to join the men or not.

Mark's deep and throaty laugh echoed down the hall. The guys sounded as if they were having fun. Suddenly she felt terribly alone. Realizing that the feeling was not likely to disappear if she remained standing in the corridor, she decided to venture in.

Mark and Artie were busy playing pool, while Dennis, Joe and Frank watched television. Taking the empty seat beside Dennis, she sat back and listened to their good-natured sparring.

"Hey, Frank." Artie's eyes held a gleam that heralded a crack at his friend's expense. "When are you going to start that diet of yours?"

"I don't need to diet. You're just jealous because God gifted me with beauty and strength."

Joe laughed. "Hey, man, if that beauty of yours gets any larger we won't need to carry hoses in our trucks anymore. We'll just roll you across the fire and smother the flames."

"Why take him at all?" Dennis leaned forward, joining in. "We'll just take his underwear. The cloth would serve as a giant fire blanket!"

"Oh, yeah?" Frank stood and switched off the TV.

Mark laughed loudly. "What a comeback. You're a real wit, Frank."

Joe turned his attention to Isabel. "As for you, I suggest putting on about thirty pounds. All in your arms, of course."

51

She was glad someone had finally included her. "We can't all have sagging biceps like you, Joe." She grinned.

Artie roared. "Atta girl. Put him in his place."

Suddenly they all stopped what they were doing. The three quick bells signaled a general alarm. Artie darted to the radio as the rest of the company scrambled for their turnout gear.

"Box Twenty-seven," he yelled as he grabbed his equipment and dashed to the pumper.

Isabel jumped on the back, taking her place next to Frank. Artie and Mark took their positions in the cab of the truck as Dennis and Joe rushed to the rescue vehicle. Sirens wailing, they raced out into the street.

Although she couldn't see Mark, Isabel knew he'd be directing their progress. By now he'd have the exact location of Box 27, as well as the whereabouts of the closest fire hydrant. Thanks to their specialized maps, which divided each section of the city into boxes, or quadrants, the process took only about twenty seconds.

Their red lights flashed brightly against the darkness of the night. The cold was biting. Suppressing the urge to let go of the handrail and turn her collar against the wind, Isabel gritted her teeth to stop their chattering. Trying to ignore her discomfort, she concentrated on the job that lay ahead.

As the pumper pulled up in front of a two-story residence, she jumped down to the pavement. The top floor was on fire and the heat had already blown out some windows.

"Take the two-and-a-half-inch," Mark yelled, pulling the air masks from the compartment on the truck.

She nodded. Taking the nozzle and three folds of hose, she began to follow him into the house. Isabel coughed as the smoke seared her lungs.

He turned around abruptly. Pulling the mask off his face briefly, he yelled, trying to be heard above the crackling of the fire around them, "Where the hell is your mask?"

She shrugged. "Back in the truck. I'll get it later." She swallowed, trying to choke back another coughing spasm.

Signaling Frank and another firefighter in the rear, he grasped her forearm roughly and pulled her back out. "Are you out of your mind? Didn't they teach you anything in the Academy?" The worried look on his face told her his anger was the result of genuine caring. "Why didn't you grab one of the masks? Didn't you realize with all the plastics inside a residence we'd probably encounter toxic fumes in there?"

She looked at him, saying nothing, waiting for the reprimand she knew she deserved. Her head ached from the cold; her eyes burned from the smoke. "I didn't want to waste any time. The quicker we went in and put out the fire, the less damage there'd be."

His fists tightened into a hard ball. "You're supposed to solve the problem, Firefighter Dailey, not become part of it!"

There was a disgusted look on his face as he shook his head. "We'll hash this out later. Let's get back to work."

Frank hurried toward them. "There's a lot of fire in two of the upstairs bedrooms. We need a man with an ax and a halligan tool to go up on the roof and cut a vent for us. The windows aren't enough to siphon all the smoke that's built up in there."

Mark muttered a curse. The cold blue eyes were snapping as they focused on her. "You think you can manage to get the ladder off the truck and then prop it against the side of the house?"

She nodded. The ladder weighed over forty

pounds. It had been one of the toughest pieces of equipment to lug around during her Academy days, but she'd managed then and she managed now.

As Mark rushed up the ladder, she followed him. Staying on the top rung of the ladder, she watched as he heaved the fire ax above his shoulders, then brought it down, smashing through roofing material. Grasping the halligan firmly in his hands, he pried the boards and shingles apart. Dark gray smoke began to escape through the hole. Isabel hoisted herself onto the roof, ready to help by relieving him of the cumbersome tools. As she stepped toward him, the roof began to tremble and sag.

Mark opened his mouth, but before he had a chance to speak, his body plummeted downward. As each layer below him collapsed, he was jerked closer to the raging inferno beneath him. Powerless to stop his descent, he shouted a warning.

Isabel scrambled forward, flattening her body against the roof. Her fingers curled tightly around Mark's collar as the final section gave way.

Mark dangled in midair, suspended only by the precarious hold she had on his jacket. Throwing her other arm forward, she secured her grasp. "I can't pull you up!" she cried.

Mark struggled to grab hold of something solid. As he did, she felt the fabric begin to slide out of her hands. "Mark, for the love of God, don't move. I can't hold on to you!"

"Let me go, then. The roof's going to collapse and you'll fall too!"

"No!" Smoke tightened its stranglehold on her throat as she struggled to breathe; heat seared her lungs, making every breath painful.

Out of nowhere two firefighters appeared. Four

powerful hands reached over her. Clutching Mark firmly under the arms, they pulled him free.

All four of them crawled back to the ladder. When they reached the bottom, the men turned to look at her.

Mark was the first to speak. "Thanks for not letting go."

Before she had a chance to reply, Dennis muttered an oath. "Loo, dammit, if she had been one of the guys, she'd have pulled you up immediately. Women shouldn't be in this job anyway. This just proves you're not cut out for this," he added, looking directly at her.

"That's not fair, Dennis. Mark weighs over two hundred pounds with all his equipment. It took both you and Frank to pull him up."

"We'll go over this later," Mark retorted flatly. "We have work to do."

Joe approached them holding a roll of bandages. "Let's take a look at those hands, Lieutenant."

"Later."

When the fire had been completely extinguished, Isabel helped Frank uncouple the hose. Draining it, they began the job of repacking. Her mind whirled. How could they blame her for not being able to pull Mark out when it had taken two of them to accomplish the job? Surely they'd see that in time.

She sighed. She was kidding herself. Dennis, and others like him, would always use it to further the argument that a woman was unfit for the job. Maybe they honestly believed it. She had to admit there was some truth in the arguments they used against her. It was possible that men like Dennis and Artie could have pulled Mark free without any help. They were exceptionally strong. On the other hand, the majority of men in the department wouldn't have fared any better than she had.

Still, no matter what the facts were, she knew she'd lost the men's respect. As far as some of them were concerned, Mark's accident had shown she lacked the physical capability to be a firefighter. Now, in order to win back their confidence, she'd have to prove her value to the department, and prove it beyond all doubt.

When they arrived at the fire station, Artie slipped out of the driver's seat and helped as Frank hung the hose over the rails of the thirty-five-foot tower. There it would remain for a few days, until it was completely dry. As each of the firefighters finished their tasks, they drifted into the kitchen, eager for a warm cup of coffee.

When everyone was present, Mark stood and faced the men. "I want everyone's attention."

Isabel sat alone, aware of the men's resentment, while the others congregated around the table.

"Firefighter Dailey could have easily let go of me when that roof began to show signs of collapsing. Instead she risked her life and stayed until help arrived. For that she's taken a lot of abuse." Mark's eyes focused on Dennis. "You're all aware of how heavy our turnout gear is. In total, I'd say I weighed about two hundred and fifty pounds. There's no way some of our guys could have pulled me out either."

Dennis' eyes showed he was unconvinced, but he said nothing.

Mark continued. "I don't want to hear another word about this incident. Is that clear?"

The men responded with a series of grunts. With a nod, Mark turned and left the room.

Isabel drained the last of her coffee, then walked

out, leaving the men to reflect on Mark's orders. Stopping by his door, she knocked lightly.

Immediately Mark appeared, his massive frame effectively blocking the doorway. "Hi! Come on in." He stepped aside. Offering her a seat, he walked to his desk. "I'm glad you're here. We have to talk."

"I know." Her eyes met his. She was completely worn-out, but still there was something about being alone with him that revitalized her sagging spirits. She watched him as he rubbed a hand over the dark stubble on his chin.

"You screwed up tonight. Then later, you held on to me and saved my neck. I'm not sure what to say."

"The incident with the mask won't happen again, Mark. I give you my word. As far as the other, I was doing my job."

His eyes held hers. "Some of our guys are going to have a hard time accepting you. It's going to be rough going for a while."

"I know." She paused briefly. "Thank you for sticking up for me."

He stood and walked to the window. Staring into the darkness, he inhaled deeply.

Isabel's eyes stayed on him. The fact that his concern was genuine didn't fail to touch her, warm her in a way nothing else could have.

"I'm going to be honest with you, Isabel," she heard him say. "Off the record, I happen to agree with the men. Women aren't suited for this job. You passed your training and that's why you're here, but what's going to happen if you ever come up against the kind of fire that goes on for hours? Those really sap your strength. Are you going to have the stamina needed to see it through? What if another firefighter's life depends on how much upper body strength you can muster?"

He paused. "I'm not referring to today. Some of our guys couldn't have pulled me up either, not without help. However, during the regular course of a fire, emergencies can crop up. All of us are paired with a 'buddy.' Is yours going to be able to depend on you to drag him to safety if necessary, particularly after you've worked the hose for hours? There's no way you can compete with a man on that score, and you know it. My suggestion is transfer out as quickly as you can. Maybe you can go into Arson Investigations or something like that. You'll be much safer there."

Isabel felt as if she had been slapped across the face. "And I thought you were different." She struggled to keep her voice even. "Not every man in this department is Hercules. Degrees of strength vary from individual to individual, as you well know. I may not be able to compete with the strongest men in our department, but I can hold my own against the rest. The fact that I made it through training proves that."

"It's true you passed, but you must admit that in this business, the more upper body strength you have, the more of an advantage it is." His tone was weary.

"In some cases, yes." She stood. "I give you my word. By the time my eight months' probation is over, you'll see that women can and do fulfill a need in this department. There are even areas where our performance can *far* outshine that of the men." She paused, determined to keep her voice steady. "I'm here to stay, Mark, and I intend to become as valuable a firefighter as any man in this department."

He exhaled slowly. "I'll be fair with you, Isabel. More than that I can't promise."

"That's all I'm asking you to do." She began walking to the door. "Good night, Mark."

"Good night."

58

4

It was early morning by the time she arrived at her apartment. Wishing she'd never heard of the Brighton Fire Department, she stepped into the living room and collapsed onto the couch with a loud sigh.

Everything was going wrong. Her father's worst predictions were coming true. For the first time she began to question the wisdom of her decision to become a firefighter.

As far back as she could remember, she had striven for her father's approval and respect, yet she had never succeeded, no matter how hard she'd tried. She realized that her decision to become a firefighter had also been motivated by the desire to please him. Instead, however, he'd treated it as an enormous joke, and the words of praise she'd hoped for never came.

Although most daughters would have turned to their mothers for comfort and attention at that point,

Isabel hadn't. She'd never had much in common with her passive, traditional-minded mom. What could she ever find in common with a woman whose entire life revolved around her home? Isabel's own beliefs and goals made them drift miles apart emotionally.

In fact she scarcely had ever enjoyed any camaraderie with other women. Even as far back as her teenage years, she'd always preferred the company of men. Their interests seemed much more challenging to her than anything the girls had to offer, but it unfortunately had left her without any female confidantes. She never really missed it, except during the long grueling months at the Academy. Only another woman would have fully understood and sympathized with the difficulties she'd faced there.

She recalled the day when she finally graduated. She'd been so proud and eager to show off to her father. She could still feel the hurt when he failed to acknowledge her accomplishment, simply ignoring it as if it hadn't happened. Even to this day, the few times he mentioned her job were always in connection with a warning that her stubbornness and insistence on doing "a man's job" were bound to cost someone his life someday.

She'd been adamant about not allowing his pessimism to affect her, scoffing at his objections and proving through carefully laid arguments that they weren't even worthy of her consideration. That's what made it even harder to accept the fact that now, through no fault of her own, the men at her station had come to the same conclusion.

She felt as if a great weight rested on her shoulders. If only they would rate her on her merits, rather than always look for her weaknesses! What hurt the most, however, was that Mark felt the same way. Even though he had sided with her, in his heart he was just like her father. Another firm believer that it was just fine for women to leave the house, as long as they came back with the groceries.

She stood and began pacing. Then again, why should she care what Mark thought of her? He had told her he'd be fair with her. His personal feelings on the subject should be of no concern to her. Still, his words had hurt her more deeply than she'd even thought possible.

A loud knocking at her door brought her back to the present. Peering out from the peephole, she saw Mark's face. She stepped aside instinctively. When would she learn to act rationally around him! She bit her lower lip thoughtfully. One thing was for certain— she wasn't prepared to deal with him now.

Noiselessly she leaned against the door. Maybe he'd go away.

The knocking sounded again. Startled, she jumped away from the door.

"Isabel, I know you're in there. I saw you get off the bus as I turned at the corner."

She grimaced. Damn! Now what?

"I can stand out here and yell until someone calls the police, or you can let me in."

"I was just about to step into the shower," she lied through the door. "Come back later."

"I just want to talk to you for a few minutes."

"Later." She tried to put as much conviction into her voice as she could.

"I'll be back."

She heard his footsteps echo down the hall. Determined to avoid any further contact with him, she decided to wait five minutes before leaving her apartment. Stopping by the mirror, she tugged at her pale green oxford shirt, letting it hang loosely outside her jeans. Brushing her hair, she waited for time to pass.

Opening the front door slightly, she peered outside. The coast was clear. This morning she'd put her free time to good use by walking to the repair shop down the street and picking up her car. She'd finally saved enough money to pay for her new transmission. With any luck, by the time she returned home, Mark would be gone. She was crossing the parking lot when a voice boomed out behind her. "Going someplace?"

She froze in her tracks.

"Good thing I decided to hang around. Were you planning to duck out on me?"

She turned around slowly. Squaring her shoulders, she looked him in the eye. "I've got to pick up my car from the garage, and I have a lot of errands to run. I'm on my own time now."

He pursed his lips. "I don't blame you for being angry, but I was just being honest with you. Are you going to hold it against me?"

"Last night you took my side in front of the men, and for that I'm grateful." Isabel's knees felt wobbly, but she fought to keep her voice steady. "As for the rest . . ." She shrugged. "I guess I'm just disappointed. I gave you more credit, and instead, you turned out to be just like the others. You concentrate on the drawbacks, treating our profession as if it's some kind of 'boys-only' club. I expected more from you." She shook her head. "And to think I was beginning to like you," she muttered absently.

He looked at her for several seconds. "For the record, Isabel, I happen to like you." He paused and added, "Quite a lot. I came over to apologize. I've been thinking about what you said, and I came to the conclusion you're right. It takes more than strength to make a good firefighter."

Isabel stared at him, unable to speak. She started to open her mouth, but stopped as he continued.

"And as far as liking me"—he gave her an arrogant smile—"you still do. That's why you're so upset."

"You conceited . . ." she sputtered, then spun on her heels and began to walk away.

Laughing, he grasped her arm and spun her around. "Peace! At any cost!"

She stared at him for several seconds. His light eyes held her spellbound. Nothing had ever prepared her for the confusion his nearness wreaked on her senses. Her throat went dry and her limbs began to tremble. "I . . ."

He cocked his head and grinned. "Good, then I'm forgiven."

"I never said . . ." She sighed. Arguing would only prolong their meeting, and right now she desperately wanted to get away from him. "Yes, you're forgiven."

"Now, tell me. How can I atone for my misdeeds?" His eyebrows shot up, giving his face a look of earnest curiosity.

She smiled slowly, thinking of the perfect way to discourage him. "Well, if you're really that eager, I'd hate to deprive you of the opportunity."

"Uh-oh."

She chuckled softly. "As a matter of fact, I was going to wallpaper my living room later today, so I can't think of a better time to have you work out some of those horrendous feelings of guilt you're having to cope with."

He groaned loudly. "I would have to open my mouth."

"Look, if you'd rather not . . ."

"No." He grinned. "Actually, it may turn out to be fun."

She blinked, surprised. "What?" She swallowed,

but continued, "I was just kidding. If you have something else to do . . ."

"Nope." He gave her a devilish grin. "Sorry I messed up your plans to sneak out on me."

"I was only going to pick up my car."

"I thought you said you were going to run a lot of errands too." He shook his head. "Tsk-tsk. Such a devious mind, and in such a lovely body."

She felt a warm flush spread over her. Shaken, and hating herself because of it, she avoided his eyes and began to walk back into the building.

"Did I hit a nerve?" His voice mocked her.

"Not at all." She tried to sound nonchalant, but something told her she hadn't fooled him.

The minute she opened her front door to let him inside, she regretted it. The apartment looked as if a hurricane had passed through. Dashing inside, she scooped up the laundry that covered the sofa and ran into the bedroom.

"I like the way you've decorated your apartment."

She emerged from the bedroom and gave him a wry smile. "Laundry thrills you, I take it."

He laughed. "I meant your paintings. Why do you always suspect the worst of me?"

She grinned back. "It saves time."

He stepped closer to a scenic vista of the Southwest desert. "You did this?"

"I used to paint quite a bit. Lately I don't seem to have much time." She stood beside him. "I've been wanting to get up to my favorite haunt and hide out with my oils and canvas for a few days, but I never seem to have a chance."

"Where's that?"

She smiled. "Should I trust you?"

"Of course. Doesn't my charming boyish face put you completely at ease?"

She laughed. "Actually . . ."

"Forget I asked," he replied with a grin. Walking to the sofa, he leaned back against the cushions and stretched his legs out. "I guess we all have places we like to run away to from time to time."

Something in his tone piqued her curiosity. "You too?"

He nodded. "I may not be an artist, but I enjoy getting away from it all. I love camping out. Being alone in the middle of nowhere with only the stars overhead can be therapeutic."

"I know what you mean," Isabel agreed. Sitting cross-legged on the opposite end of the couch, she faced him. "If I had a choice, I'd live in the middle of the country instead of the city." She shrugged, then smiled. "Brighton was my idea of a compromise. It's not a bustling metropolis, but I can still earn a living."

"Brighton is as large a city as I care to live in too. I just wish it would stop growing. Do you realize that in the past few years it's almost doubled in size? Just two years ago there were farms and meadows up and down the river valley. Now it's all housing developments."

"I know. I hate to see subdivisions cropping up everywhere. It's depressing when there are look-alike houses as far as the eye can see."

His eyes had a distant look. "I'll tell you one thing. If I ever do get married, I'll never live in a tract house. My idea of home is someplace where I'll have a little elbow room around me. I want at least an acre around my place."

"Do you ever picture yourself married?" Her curiosity overpowered her desire to remain cautiously aloof.

"I must admit that it takes all the imagination I've

got to picture myself with a wife and kids." He looked at her and grinned.

She stood quickly. "I think we better get to work. It's going to be a long, hard job. The paper I liked wasn't prepasted, so it's going to make it just a bit more difficult."

He groaned.

Isabel laughed softly. "Remember. You volunteered." She walked to the hall closet and began to extract the tools they'd need. "I'll be honest. I'm grateful to have your help. I've been putting this off, not wanting to tackle it on my own and end up wallpapering myself to a light fixture or something. I've never done this before, and although the instruction booklet didn't make it sound difficult, it also didn't sound like it was going to be a snap."

"Well, have no fear, as they say." He joined her and helped her carry the supplies to the center of the living room. "I've never done this either, but I'm sure it isn't that complicated."

She stopped in mid-step. "You've never done this . . ." She looked at him warily. "But your apartment is almost completely wallpapered. The way the colors match your furniture, I assumed . . ."

"I hired a college student to do it for me," he answered simply.

"In that case, I think we're in trouble." Isabel sighed.

"Look at it as an adventure. Just because we haven't done it before doesn't mean it has to be a disaster. We'll make a great team." He gave her a mischievous grin.

She feigned great concentration on the wallpaper pattern. If only his looks didn't tempt her so! She couldn't help but wonder what it would be like to feel his arms around her, or have his lips cover hers. . . .

Looking up and seeing his eyes resting on her, she felt a warm telltale flush spread over her skin.

"Penny for your thoughts?" His grin told her he'd made an accurate guess.

She felt torn between the urge to say something outrageous and shatter his facade of cool self-confidence, and the need to relax and let fate lead them where it may. Instead she just pointed to the instruction booklet and picked up the trimming knife, then knelt to unroll a length of wallpaper.

"Right." Picking up the booklet, he began leafing through it. "Give me a chance to skim over this before we start."

Several minutes later, he closed the pamphlet and tossed it aside. "It won't be that difficult. The hardest part is going to be matching the pattern." He crouched behind her and placed his hands on her shoulders. "You *would* pick stripes."

The warmth of his hands flowed through the light fabric of her blouse, igniting her skin, and making her painfully aware of his touch. A mixture of desire and apprehension washed over her. Unable to stem the tide of emotions, and angry at herself because of her inability to do so, Isabel stood and walked several steps away from him. "The super let me borrow a piece of plywood that's long enough for us to stretch out the paper while we brush the paste on. We're going to have to work on the floor, so we need to spread newspapers beneath the board so we protect the rug."

"Sounds like a good idea. There's only one problem as far as I can see."

She gave him a quizzical look.

"If you're going to jump every time I touch you, we're going to be laying out a very interesting pattern on your wall."

She swallowed. Squaring her shoulders and mustering as much dignity as she could, she met his unwavering gaze. "I don't understand what you're talking about."

"I think you do." Mark's lips curved in an arrogant smile.

Her throat constricted and she clenched her hands to keep them from trembling as his mesmeric blue eyes held her spellbound. With unwilling fascination Isabel watched as he approached. The air caught in her lungs was suffocating, yet something prevented her from taking a step backward.

His gaze held hers as his hands reached to the nape of her neck and curved, stroking her. "I'm not the enemy, you know," he said in a low voice. "It's all right to let your guard down."

She knew what his next move would be, but did nothing to prevent it. She saw the gentle glow in his eyes as he closed the gap between them. His lips trailed a downward path from her forehead, tasting in sweet exploration, savoring her with the agonizingly slow pace of an experienced lover. With seductive persuasion he dragged his tongue temptingly over her lips. Avoiding the invitation her parted mouth offered, with extraordinary forbearance he molded her to suit his whim, increasing the incendiary passions coursing through her.

Longing, more deeply embedded than caution, surged to the surface. Unable to passively wait for the kiss she knew would eventually be hers, Isabel sought his mouth with fierce abandon.

Mark laughed softly, a deep throaty laugh that acknowledged his victory. "Now perhaps you'll be able to understand how badly I've wanted you."

She should have pushed him away, but that would

have put an end to the delicious sensations he created, leaving her giddy with want. "Mark . . ." Her voice sounded strange, so unlike her own.

His mouth crashed over hers. With a soft moan she strained against him, entwining her fingers around the richness of his thick brown hair. Her lips parted eagerly, inviting him further. Yet the inducement was hardly needed as his tongue plundered her with a probing ferocity that left her reverberating against him. She held back nothing as he fed her hunger with skillful mastery that awakened new fires within her soul.

Without freeing her mouth, he stepped back, allowing enough room between them to give his hands the full freedom of her body. Pushing his way gently beneath the fabric of her blouse, he caressed the skin below, moving everywhere, yet lingering nowhere. Her senses reeled under the thoroughness of his touch. Undoing the clasp of her brassiere with one expert motion, he explored the valley between her breasts; then his hands slipped downward. His roughened palms pressed against her ribs, then once again moved up, stopping as they reached the undercurve of her breasts. He cradled the soft flesh gently, allowing the warmth of his touch to work its persuasive magic on her senses.

She moaned softly, writhing against him with unresolved longing. In the face of a rapidly fading reality, she fought to regain her sanity. Concentrating on all she disliked about him, trying to find the will to pull away, she searched for a way to shatter the spell he wove around her.

He eased his embrace slightly. "You're still fighting me, Isabel. Can't you sense the futility in that?"

The words caught in her throat. She wanted to

scream at him to stop, to leave her apartment and never come back, yet the protest died before it was ever voiced.

"I want to make love to you. Give yourself to me, sweetheart. Trust me to take care of you."

"I can't." Her voice sounded weak. "I don't want to. . . ."

"Yes, you do," he murmured in her ear.

Her own needs were betraying her, turning her into easy prey. She was being seduced, she knew, yet was doing nothing to stop it.

"I want to make love to you, Isabel, slowly and very thoroughly. I won't spare any part of you at all. I'll make you respond to me in ways you never even knew existed. You'll be mine, sweetheart, but you don't have to be afraid. You see, it won't be a one-way street. I'll be yours in return."

"You don't understand me," she whispered in a low tortured voice. She wanted him more than she'd ever thought possible, yet with that feverish need came an elusive fear. He had awakened a slumbering passion within her, one that could engulf her in its searing flames, leaving nothing but ashes behind.

"You're wrong. I do understand. That attraction you felt toward me when we first met has grown. You care a great deal about me. What you've refused to see is that you're very special to me too."

Did he really feel that way, or was she being swayed by the fact that she wanted so desperately to believe him? The question tore at her, snapping her back to reality. "Don't lie to me, Mark." She pushed away. "I heard you talking to your friend that day I was at your apartment. I'm just a challenge—nothing more, nothing less."

He grasped her arm firmly. "You're wrong. *He* might have thought that, but it wasn't true then, and it isn't true now." His hand caressed the side of her face shaping it's contours. Instinctively Isabel tilted her head, resting it against his outstretched palm. He smiled gently at her, then pulled her back into his arms.

"I admit," he murmured against her hair, "the attraction I feel for you hasn't made it easy for me, particularly when we're at work. I don't want to be overprotective, yet it's instinctive. I don't want anything to hurt you. I tried to ignore my feelings, but it didn't work. You're in my thoughts constantly, Isabel, and unless I'm very mistaken, I think you feel the same way about me."

"I don't know how I feel." She pushed away from him.

He pulled her gently yet firmly back against him. "I think you do. You just don't want to admit it."

"I don't want to get entangled with a man like you, Mark. Get out of my life!" Isabel's voice rose, giving her tone an almost desperate quality, as she shook herself free.

"If I thought you really meant that, I'd leave right now." Mark stepped closer to her, standing only inches away from her.

"Then go." She lowered her voice and averted her gaze from his eyes, staring longingly at the muscular chest that had been her haven minutes ago.

"The problem is that I know you're lying, Isabel." He took another step toward her. His arms wrapped around her waist, pulling her toward him and molding her against him. "Even now, as I hold you, you're trembling. You want me to love you, and you want to love me. You're simply afraid. And, sweetheart, you have nothing to fear from me."

"But I do," she said softly, wishing she could explain, yet knowing she could not.

"Look at me, Isabel." Mark's voice was deep, sensual, and infinitely persuasive.

She refused, knowing that if she did, her power to resist him would fade away.

"Look at me," he repeated softly.

The strength of the arms that held her prisoner, the heady masculine scent of him, the promise he held out to her, all combined to overwhelm her senses in a blaze of primitive sexual desire. She wanted this man to love her, to take her and make her one with him.

5

Stirrings more powerful than any Isabel had ever known came to life, engulfing her, demanding to be satisfied.

Mark tilted her chin toward him and she felt herself drowning in the intensity of his blue gaze. There would be no escape. His tongue flicked at the moist corners of her mouth until her lips parted obligingly. His hand roamed unchecked and circled her breast as his kiss deepened, turning into a fevered exploration that robbed her of the will to resist.

Pushing her blouse from her shoulders, he bared her to the waist, then savored the sight before him. "You're so lovely." He kissed the sloping hollow of her neck, then her shoulder. His descending mouth tantalized her with an intoxicating promise while his palms slid over her breasts.

She moaned, arching toward him, her hips beginning to sway in a subtle yearning motion. Molding herself against him, she sought contact with the powerful force of his maleness, confined only by a thin strip of cloth.

He shuddered. "Oh, Lord, Isabel." Without hesitation he lifted her off her feet and carried her through the open doorway leading to her bedroom.

He laid her gently on the bed, then unsnapped her slacks and pulled them off. His work-roughened palm caressed the flat of her belly, then in one quick motion divested her of the last bit of clothing that stood in his way.

His hand roamed in a fleeting caress over her. Wild under his touch, she tugged at the buttons of his shirt, then slid her hand inside the open front. She curled her fingers in the chestnut hair and found his skin almost hot to her touch.

He buried his lips in her waist, then left a moist, fiery trail of kisses as he explored her length. As his palm slid downward, he sought her parted lips once more. He invaded her mouth at the same instant his hand reached a more intimate goal. The contact was electric. Isabel gasped as shock waves ripped through her. Her emotions careened and clashed, leaving her body reverberating with desire. Her fists clenched against his chest as her hips strained against the incendiary movement of his hand.

Fire raced in her blood as her fingers moved to curl around the base of his neck and pull him closer to her. His parted mouth plundered her nakedness, leaving no area untouched as she writhed, helpless with a passion that would not be quenched. The gentle flicking of his tongue felt like hot brands.

He allowed her a brief respite as he stood and divested himself of all his clothing. She watched, fascinated by the strong curve of his limbs and the powerful maleness that jutted with unabashed desire. He stood, letting her study him, then lowered himself gently over her.

Isabel felt his heart beat against the nakedness of her breasts; then he buried himself in her, thrusting into the warm intimate recesses she had withheld from him.

Her body yielded to him, quivering with longing and expectation. Filling her with the force of his masculine power, he moved with deliberate slowness. His tempo increased as her body closed in around him. Slipping a hand beneath her, he controlled her movements and locked her body against his.

Propelled into a world of explosive sensations, Isabel sought nothing, giving herself instead to a surrender so total that her whole universe seemed to vibrate with love. Drifting in an ethereal light, she gloried in the rich kaleidoscope of colors unfolding before her eyes. As she clung to him, still quivering from the aftershock, she felt a curious sense of peace settling over her.

He rolled over, taking her with him. Positioning her so her head rested on his chest, he smoothed her sweat-dampened locks, pushing them away from her forehead. "Do you see now how good it can be between us?"

She didn't answer as reality slowly returned to the cocoon of contentment that sweetly enveloped her. With a sigh, she snuggled deeper into his arms.

"I wish we could stay just as we are now for the rest of our lives," Mark whispered gently.

"Nice, but not very practical," Isabel teased in a soft voice as she ran her fingers through the thick curly hair on his chest. "We'd starve in a few weeks."

"Oh, I suppose we could run to the refrigerator once or twice a day, just to keep up our strength and stamina."

"Speaking of strength and stamina . . ." She propped herself up on one elbow and smiled. "I think we have some unfinished business out in the living room."

"I was afraid you were going to think of that sooner or later," Mark replied. "Why couldn't it have been later?"

"If I haven't totally exhausted you, how about helping me finish up out there?"

He exhaled loudly. "No time like the present, right?"

Slipping out of bed, she grabbed his shirt from where it had been tossed, and put it on, fastening a few buttons to hold it in place. "There, I'm ready for wallpapering. And you can work with your shirt off, so I won't be deprived either."

Laughing, Mark got out of bed and slipped into his trousers. "What if you get paste all over my nice new shirt? You look like the clumsy type."

"Then I guess I'll never take the shirt off again," she said, grinning.

Taking her hand in his, he led her into the living room. "All right. Let's finish that wallpapering of yours."

Half-clothed, they both set to work clearing the space around the walls. Isabel concentrated on enjoying their day off together, temporarily banishing her reservations about Mark and their relationship.

A half-hour later they were ready to begin the final phase of their work. Isabel held the first strip of paper flat while Mark began brushing paste onto the back.

"So you've never done this before?" Isabel inquired. "Most of the firemen I've met are handymen around the house. A lot of them helped build their own houses."

"Don't you think I've demonstrated my handiness enough already today?" Mark laughed. "Actually," he continued, "I've constructed several fireplaces and foundations for other firemen. Stonework really appeals to me. There's a lot of satisfaction in building something that lasts."

"Then we do have something in common. I feel the same way about things that are lasting." She looked him straight in the eye, for emphasis.

He paused, and met her gaze. Her meaning had not been lost on him.

Finishing a few hours later, they stood back and admired their work.

"It came out nicely, I'd say, considering it's our first time." His tone made it plain that his words had more than one meaning.

"Adequate," she replied, trying to keep a straight face.

"The word you're looking for is 'memorable.'" Mark's eyes pierced through her, reading her thoughts with the perception of a clairvoyant.

As she turned away from him, she heard his voice behind her: "You look so tempting wearing nothing but my shirt." Then suddenly his arms encircled her waist, pulling her back against him. His trousered legs rubbed against her naked ones, sending a shiver coursing down her spine. His outstretched palms moved upward, gently cupping her breasts. "See how they mold and conform to me?" He nuzzled her neck.

A familiar languorous feeling swept over her in waves. "Why does love have such a high price?" She pulled away from him in horror, realizing she had spoken the thought out loud.

Grasping her shoulders, he turned her around until

she faced him. "I think it's time we had a serious talk about our relationship."

She fought the rising tide of panic that engulfed her. "I don't think we should," she said hesitantly.

"I want to know exactly where we stand, Isabel. Don't you think you owe me at least that much?"

She nodded, then led him to the couch. "I heard you say once that you didn't believe in marriage." Would she scare him off and thus end the conflict inside herself? Nothing seemed easy. She didn't want to lose him: just the thought caused her heart to constrict. But what price would she have to pay if he stayed? Was she willing to risk losing herself in order to keep him?

"If you're hoping I'll give you an easy way out, Isabel, then you're in for a disappointment. My feelings for you are much too real and much too strong to let you just walk away from me. For the first time in my life I'm beginning to think that love isn't only an abstract emotion, one that I'm simply not capable of. You've turned my whole life around and I'm not going to let you slip away. At least not without a fight."

She felt torn between the need to melt into his arms and the urge to run away as fast and as far as she could. "I'm not sure we're right for each other, Mark. Try to understand. I won't deny the attraction that exists between us—"

"Attraction?" His voice rose. "Haven't you heard a word I've said? I think I'm falling in love with you!" He glared at her, his blue eyes blazing. "And don't try telling me that you have no feelings for me. The look in your eyes when I kiss you, the way you tremble when I hold you—those are the signs of a woman in love, aren't they?"

"I . . ." What could she say? Instinct told her that Mark would be a part of her forever. She wanted to love him, she wanted to let go of herself, yet a nameless fear held her back each time. Love didn't always enhance. It had turned her mother into little more than a robot whose sole function was to please her father.

Mark had the same inner strength, and her feelings for him were overpowering at times. How could she explain her fear? How could she tell him feelings this intense could end up destroying her, that taking a risk like that required more than she was able to give?

He stared at her silently, lost in thought. When he spoke, his voice was no more than a whisper. "It's caring for me that terrifies you so, isn't it?"

Why was the truth so hard to deny? She swallowed; then, fighting to keep her voice steady, she glanced up at him and spoke. "I don't want to live my life the way my mother lived hers," she replied truthfully.

"All I know about your family is that your dad was the former chief. He retired a few years ago, didn't he?"

She opened her mouth as if to speak, then closed it, shaking her head. "Telling you won't serve any purpose."

He leaned forward and grabbed her arm gently, pulling her back down into her chair. "Don't shut me out. Talk to me." His voice was hushed, filled with a tenderness she couldn't resist.

Reluctantly she began to speak. "I've never met anyone like you, Mark. You've shown me just how wonderful being a woman can be." She took her hand away from his, needing to concentrate solely on what she had to say. "But I just can't let this go any further. I don't want to get involved with anyone, especially a firefighter, at least not yet.

"I know the risks involved in our profession. I also saw what my mother went through every time my father was late coming home from work." She looked up into his eyes and almost lost her thought. "You're a lot like my dad. You have very definite ideas of what a woman should and shouldn't do. To get further involved with you is going to cost me—the more I give to you, the more you'll expect. I just don't think I'm ready to live the rest of my life that way. At least not the way I feel now."

He reached across the table and brushed the hair from her eyes. It was a simple gesture of tenderness, yet it coursed through her like an electric shock. "Aren't you judging me prematurely?"

"Maybe," she acknowledged, "but I can't help the way I feel. You asked me to tell you why I was holding back."

He gave her a speculative look. "I think there's more, something that you're not saying." His eyes narrowed slightly. "Are you afraid that your feelings for me will somehow end up changing you into someone you won't like?"

Slowly she nodded.

"Then you still have a lot to learn about me." He stood. "I won't beg you to give our relationship a chance. It isn't something I can force on you." He paused. "From this point on, it'll be up to you. If you decide what we have is worth taking a chance on, then come to me and let me know. I'll wait." He paused again, then added, "But not forever."

She looked at him, her hands damp. "Is that your way of putting pressure on me?" she challenged.

"No," he replied evenly. "I'm just not big on hopeless causes. You and I care a great deal for each other. I want you to realize that if we start going out, it's going to mean more than a series of casual dates. If you're aware of that and you come freely to me, we'll both know that our goals are one and the same."

Silently she gazed at him, pleading for understanding, hoping somehow he'd understand.

"You don't know what you want, do you?" Mark's voice was deep; it's timbre sent vibrations to her core. "All right. Take the time you need to sort out your thoughts. Just keep one thing in mind. I'm not your father and you're not your mother. Being similar in some ways doesn't make us identical." He studied her for a second. "Isabel, no one can change you if you won't let them. Besides, I'd be the last person on earth who'd want to see that happen. By falling in love with you, and turning you into someone else, I'd only be cheating myself."

The words burned in her mind, but the fear remained.

The following week at work, Mark seemed to take special care to avoid her. He seldom spoke to her unless it was on a matter of business. The strain was beginning to wear on her. Several times she had wanted to go to him and put an end to differences that kept them apart, but she couldn't. By giving in now, she'd only be proving that her feelings for him would, in the end, be her undoing. She'd start making compromise after compromise until she'd scarcely know the person she'd become. Wasn't that precisely what her mother had done?

So she remained silent and concentrated on other problems plaguing her at work. The other firefighters, having had time to mull over the events surrounding Mark's near-accident, had begun to see that she wasn't to blame. Dennis, however, still remained staunch in his opposition to her. Unfortunately the men held him in high regard, and his opinion could always be counted to sway the others. It worried her. Dennis could make things very difficult for her if he chose. If only she could prove to him that she was right, that there really was a place for women in the department.

As she finished waxing the ladder truck, she stood back and admired her work. It had taken over three hours, but the truck was now spotless. Satisfied, she walked to the kitchen, ready for a much-earned coffee break.

The room was empty save for Dennis, who sat by the table studying a firefighting manual. Cursing her luck, she stood by the doorway, trying to decide if she should go inside or turn around and avoid him.

Dennis looked up, then wordlessly glanced back down at the manual.

Isabel took a deep breath and walked inside. "Hello."

She received no answer.

As she poured herself a cup of coffee, she stared at her cup pensively. Would it be better to leave Dennis alone, or should she take the opportunity to talk things out with him, now that they were by themselves? She peered at him furtively out of the corner of her eye. He already disapproved of her. What did she have to lose by confronting him?

She went across the room and sat in the chair opposite him. "Dennis, I want to talk to you."

He looked up. His glance was cold enough to make a polar bear shiver. "What do you want?"

"You've been making my life very difficult lately. I know you wish the department had never allowed women in, but can't you at least try to be fair? I'm not asking for any special favors, mind you, all I want is for you to withhold judgment on me until you have more to go on. Once enough time passes, you'll be in a position to more accurately gauge what my capabilities and my weaknesses really are."

"It's not a matter of passing judgment, Isabel." With an air of resignation he closed the manual. "I just happen to think that without the strength you can't do the job properly. I don't want to see someone lose his life simply because his backup was unable to perform her duties."

"I may not be as strong as you are, but I'm not weak either. I've been able to keep up with most of the men in the department. My abilities are yet to be proved. Be patient. If I really don't have what it takes, I won't make it past probation."

"And what will the cost of finding that out be? Have you thought that through?"

She met his glare with an unblinking gaze. "First of all, as a probie my responsibilities are very limited. You know I'll be supervised all the time, particularly while working fires. To speculate on the 'what if' isn't going to get us anywhere. It's obvious we don't agree on this. Getting into an argument isn't going to make things better."

"I didn't bring it up."

"No, I had to, because you've forced the issue. You know darn well how much the men value your opinion. Like any other recruit, I have a lot of things to learn and a lot of problems to contend with. Don't make it even more difficult for me by turning everyone against me."

"I think you overestimate my influence."

"I wish I did," she replied honestly. "The fact is, the others were starting to realize that the incident with Mark was not a fair test of my abilities. Most of our guys couldn't have pulled him up either. Everything would have returned to normal if you hadn't started putting more questions in their minds."

He leaned back in his chair and studied her. "I'm entitled to my opinion."

She stood. "Yes, but can't you keep that opinion to yourself until you have more to base it on? You'd extend that courtesy to any other new firefighter. Won't you at least do the same for me?"

He considered the question. "Yes, I can do that, but if the guys ask me for my opinion, I'm not going to lie to them."

"I wouldn't expect you to—just don't volunteer it with such alarming frequency."

Dennis looked at her and began to laugh. "Your point is well taken. I'll try to keep my mouth shut. Fair enough?"

She smiled and nodded. "Fair enough."

He stood. "Now, if you don't mind, I'm going back to my bunk and get some studying done. I'm trying to pass the paramedic's exam."

"In that case, Firefighter Dennis Kerry"—she gave him a slight bow—" be my guest." She smiled. "And if you need someone to test you, someone who'll ask you the hardest possible questions, give me a call. I'll be more than happy to provide that service."

"I just bet you would." He laughed. "And that might be a real help."

"Anytime." She smiled.

Isabel returned to her seat and made herself comfortable. Picking up a magazine someone had left behind, she began to leaf through it. Suddenly she spotted movement out of the corner of her eye. Turning her head abruptly, she found herself staring at a perfectly proportioned slender male hip. She gulped, and her eyes drifted upwards, stopping for a fraction of a second to stare at the muscular torso and the hair-darkened triangular patch the collar of his workshirt exposed. She didn't need to see his face to know who it was.

"Mark." Her voice cracked.

He grinned. "I was standing just outside the doorway when you were talking to Dennis. You handled that situation very well."

Her blood ran hot, barely registering his words. Almost as if he knew the effect his proximity was having on her, he stood his ground and smiled.

"Aren't you going to say anything?"

"What?" She choked. "I mean, thank you."

He laughed. "Is something distracting you, Firefighter Dailey?"

Angered by his mocking tone, she pretended to shift her attention back to the magazine. "I was just reading this article."

He laughed. "That's some article."

She started to turn her head again, but stopped halfway. "What do you mean?"

"Who'd have thought you'd find a two-page cigarette ad so enthralling?"

She looked down quickly and gasped. Damn him! "I was just about to turn the page."

His laugh's throaty timbre echoed its way into her heart. "What a horrible liar you are."

She stood abruptly, meaning to walk past him, but he stepped to the side and blocked her way. Her heart palpitated wildly as the heat radiating from his body washed gently over her.

He grazed her cheek with his palm. "You're so beautiful when you have that look about you."

"What look?" Her eyebrows furrowed.

"The one of a woman who wants very much to be made love to."

She tried to answer, but the words got caught in her throat.

"Don't make us wait too much longer, Isabel." His voice was low and husky, its quality filling her with treacherous expectancy.

Her heart leaped to her throat. She wanted to rebuke him, to say anything that would shatter that implacable, smug exterior, but before she had a chance to reply, he turned and walked out.

Cursing herself for never being able to think of the perfect rejoinder when she needed it, instead of two days later, she muttered an angry oath and kicked the leg of the table. With a yelp, she jumped back, holding her foot in one hand.

Muffled laughter came from the doorway.

Planting both feet firmly back on the ground and pretending her toes didn't hurt at all, she turned toward the sound. Mark's face peered around the door, grinning widely.

"I can think of better ways to work out pent-up frustrations." With a wink, he strode down the hall.

Isabel closed her eyes and shook her head. She hated Mark Grady. That was all there was to it. She sighed. Who was she kidding? He was practically all she could think about. Of all the men she could have picked, why did she have to fall in love with him? *In love.* The thought jolted her.

She slumped back into her chair. Now what? Should she continue to fight him, or should she allow herself to care for him despite the cost of allowing their relationship to grow? The way Mark had set things up between them, it was clearly an all-or-nothing proposition. If she went to him, then she'd have to admit she was ready to commit herself—at least to the point of seriously trying to carve out a future for themselves. She didn't want to let him go, but the alternative was equally frightening.

She thought of her mother. Was she also destined to lead a life that revolved around someone else? Was she really capable of setting all her hopes and all her dreams aside so that Mark's might be fulfilled? She shook her head. That might have happened to her mother, but it would never happen to her.

Her future would be spent with a man who could give her security without feeling threatened by her accomplishments. Any man who demanded as much from her as Mark did would sooner or later increase his pressure until he had molded her into precisely what he wanted. The problem, however, lay in her own weakness. Eager to please him, she'd soon find herself capitulating time after time. Life with him would mean no life at all for her.

No. She couldn't settle for that. Angrily she walked down the corridor to her bunk.

Isabel waited in the kitchen as the other members of the platoon strolled inside. Within a few minutes their informal briefing session would begin. Mark sat alone on the table. With his attention riveted on the notebook before him, he seemed oblivious of everything and everyone else. She watched him for several seconds, her heart full of a nameless longing.

As the firefighters began to congregate, she diverted her attention to the gathering crowd. Dennis leaned against the counter sipping a cup of coffee while Artie and Frank sat astride their chairs. Knowing the meeting would start at precisely seven-thirty, Isabel glanced around, picked out an empty seat and made herself comfortable.

Seconds later Mark stood, turned to the men and began. "As of tomorrow we start day shift. Everyone is expected to arrive at the station by eight o'clock to relieve his counterpart on the night shift."

Artie groaned. "I hate day shifts."

"I'm afraid it goes with the territory, Artie, my boy." Mark smiled. "Unfortunately, since we're still having manpower shortages, our schedule is also a bit off. We'll have only today off, or what's left of it after we get out of here this morning, before starting a ten-hour, five-day workweek."

A loud groan went around the room.

"Come on, guys," he chided good-naturedly, "it isn't exactly as if we're going to be answering call after call. Day shifts, as you well know, can be pretty slow sometimes."

"Boring, you mean," Dennis added with a grin.

"Okay. Have it your way." Mark laughed. "Boring."

"After we finish the five-day stint, what then?" Artie asked.

"We get three days off, then another week consisting of fourteen-hour night shifts."

Frank Lindsey stood and poured himself a cup of coffee. "When's the City Council going to allocate more funds for our department? I don't mind the overtime, but . . ." He left the sentence hanging.

"I'm not sure," Mark answered candidly. "From what I've heard, there's no immediate end in sight. They did a study that averaged the number of calls received by each of our stations, and the number they came up with was seven. They figured that at that rate we can handle things indefinitely."

"Peachy," Frank muttered sarcastically.

"It won't be so bad," Isabel interjected. "I mean, if we really don't have that many calls—"

"Spoken like a true probie," Dennis muttered loud enough for everyone to hear.

The sound of laughter rippled across the room.

She felt her face burn. "All I meant—"

Mark laughed. "Come on, guys. Quit picking on the lady."

Isabel looked down at her shoes, too uncomfortable

to meet the gazes aimed in her direction. There had been a protectiveness in his tone she hoped the others hadn't heard. She gathered her courage and looked around. Everyone's attention had now returned to Mark. Had she only imagined the special nuance in his voice?

As their replacements began to arrive at the station, Mark called an end to the meeting. "That's it for now. Make sure you're all on time tomorrow."

Isabel left the substation quickly, hoping to avoid running into Mark. She had to find a way to get him out of her thoughts, to stop the feelings she had for him! The leisurely drive home provided no answers. She was just getting out of her car when she spotted him standing in front of her building. For a brief second she considered running away, but at that same instant he spotted her. With a casual wave he walked to her side.

"Hello." There was a penetrating warmth in his gaze.

"Mark, what are you doing here?" Afraid he'd spot the nervous confusion on her face, she concentrated on maintaining a facade of relaxed indifference. "Is there something I can help you with?" Not wanting to ask him inside her apartment, she stood by the sidewalk and waited.

"Actually, yes."

Why had she asked? "Problems?"

"A minor one, really, but I need your help."

"What's up?" It sounded legitimate. Maybe she was overreacting.

"I was supposed to give a talk about what it's like to be a firefighter at one of our high schools, but I have a meeting with the chief and I can't make it. Were you planning to do anything special today?"

"Not really." She shrugged. "I thought I'd finish a

painting I was doing for my father's birthday, then go jogging this afternoon."

"I know it's short notice"—he grinned sheepishly—"actually no notice, but do you think you can take over for me with the kids?"

"I don't know how good I'll be at this, but I'm willing to give it a try," she ventured slowly. "Where do I have to go and what time should I be there?"

"Be at Franklin High"—he checked his watch—"in an hour."

"All right."

"I better get going too. I got the chief's call after everyone left the station, so I drove back here hoping I'd be able to catch you at home." He jammed his hands into his pockets. "It took you a lot longer than I expected."

"I went for a drive. I had some things to sort out . . ." She stopped abruptly, realizing she had explained too much.

He smiled. "I hope you came to the right decision."

"Mark . . ." She averted her eyes, hating the way her heart leaped every time he smiled.

"Haven't made up your mind yet?" he teased good-naturedly. "Why don't you just admit you're in love with me? It'll make things so much simpler."

"It doesn't make things simpler at all."

"Why not?"

"Never mind." She sighed. "Go to your meeting."

"Tell me what you meant first."

"No," she said stubbornly.

He checked his watch and muttered an oath. "Give me a hint?"

"No."

"Be that way, then." He leaned over. Taking her by surprise, he sealed her lips in a bruising kiss. "That's to let you know what you're missing."

Her lips were still throbbing as he turned and ran toward his car. "See you later, beautiful."

She watched him from the sidewalk, unable to will away the electric sense of awareness his body had left on hers. An unbearable sadness mingled with a tension she couldn't explain. Her stomach suddenly felt as if she had swallowed a large lump of clay.

Was she more like her mother than she cared to admit even to herself? Of all the men in the world, why had she picked Mark to get involved with?—the one man who'd take absolute possession of her soul!

Yet, was she ready to face the alternative? Could she give him up now that he had insinuated himself into her life, into her heart? He had made it abundantly clear he wouldn't wait forever. It was now up to her.

Slowly she walked inside the building and into her apartment.

6

•◦◦◦◦◦◦◦◦◦◦•

Isabel sat in her apartment enjoying the time alone. Giving a lecture on what it was like to be a firefighter had turned out to be much harder than she had anticipated. Initially she'd planned to give an informal talk on training and requirements, then hold a ten-or fifteen-minute question-and-answer session. She'd intended to spend about a half-hour at the high school.

Some dreamer she'd turned out to be! The class had ended over an hour later. A few of the kids who didn't have another class scheduled immediately after had lagged behind, deluging her with questions. She hadn't minded; their interest was flattering in many ways. Still, by the time she got home, she felt glassy-eyed and mentally exhausted.

For forty minutes she had done little except sip a cola with her feet propped up on the coffee table. Feeling relaxed and more than just a little lazy, she rested her head against the back of the couch and closed her eyes.

The next sound she heard was a loud knocking at her door. Startled, her eyes popped open.

The knocking sounded again.

Levering herself up, she walked to the door. Mark's face greeted her. "How did it go?"

"Just fine." She gave him a drowsy smile.

"Did I wake you?" He sounded concerned, but not overly so.

"Actually, I'm glad you did. I've got several things I wanted to do this afternoon, and sleeping away my entire day off wasn't exactly what I had in mind."

He cocked his head to one side. "Aren't you going to ask me in?"

More awake than she had been, she gave him a wary look. "Are you going to behave?"

He laughed. "If I must."

She stepped aside and waved him into the apartment. "Care for a soft drink?"

He shook his head. "I've been thinking about us most of the morning, and I've got a solution."

The words jolted her consciousness with an impact she hadn't anticipated. Was he going to force the issue? What should she say? She watched him warily. He'd rolled up the sleeves of his madras shirt, revealing hair-darkened forearms. His black twill jeans fit snugly, accentuating slim hips. She swallowed. Why was her apartment so infernally hot all of a sudden? A casual glance at the thermostat, that unconscionable traitor, revealed her air conditioner was working well and the temperature was a cool sixty-eight degrees. Isabel shifted nervously.

Mark's lips curved into a sensual, self-confident smile. Sitting down comfortably on her sofa, arms outstretched on the back of the couch, he watched her.

She sat on one of the side chairs. Even at that distance, his voice and his nearness combined to weave a spell around her that robbed her of reason. Fighting the urge to go to him and melt into his arms, she gripped the arms of the chair so tightly that her hands were partially numbed.

Noting her tension, Mark shook his head. "What am I going to do with you?"

She raised one eyebrow quizzically. "Have I confused you that much? You seemed to have a definite plan of action when you came in."

"Come sit beside me." He patted the empty cushion on his right.

"I can hear you perfectly well from here," she replied tersely.

"All right, if you're going to be stubborn about it." Mark spoke each word slowly, making each syllable drip with mock resignation.

"What did you want to tell me?" Her voice sounded winded. Had she been holding her breath?

His gaze was steady and assessing. "I have an idea that's going to make life a lot simpler for both of us."

Her heart constricted. Unable to move, she stared at him, waiting for him to continue.

"You're not ready to make any kind of commitment right now, and as I've told you already, I'm going to give you enough time to sort out your thoughts. In the meantime, however, I think we should remain friends."

"Oh, of course!" She leaned forward. "I never meant for us not to be—"

"Wait, you haven't heard the rest of it."

She leaned back in her chair slowly. The rest of it?

What more could he have to say? Lapsing into an uneasy silence, she watched him. The blood pounded fiercely in her ears, and her entire body felt rigid.

"I want us to continue seeing each other. I realize the way things worked out before, we were in a no-win situation. I'd asked you not to come to me unless you were willing to commit yourself to a relationship—but how can you make that decision unless we see each other regularly?"

"Well, you do have a point—"

"Let me finish." He paused, then continued. "What I propose is this: let's start all over again as friends. Let's just relax and let this relationship take its natural course. We'll go out and share all the things good friends do, without pressuring each other. What do you say?"

She was well aware that by agreeing to see him on a regular basis the depth of her feelings for him would grow steadily, careening her over the brink of safety. It was not a suitable alternative. "All right," she heard herself say.

"Good." He stood, then walked to her door. "Did you have any plans for tonight?"

She shook her head, afraid to trust her voice.

"Good. I'll pick you up at seven."

"Why?" She shut her eyes and turned her head. Insecurity washed over her in waves that left her feeling inadequate. *Isabel, try not to act like more of an idiot than you have to.*

"One of the lieutenants from Engine Company Fifty-two is having a get-together at his house. I thought you might like to meet some of the other guys in the department."

"I would?" Embarrassed, she shook her head and added staunchly, "Of course I would!"

"So seven o'clock's okay with you?" His eyes shone with a devilish amusement.

"Sure," she said, failing miserably to sound casual in the face of the full power of his charm.

"Good. Dress casually. I'll pick you up later." He took one step toward her.

For a brief expectant minute Isabel thought he was going to kiss her. Her pulse began to pound at an alarming rate as she waited for him to close the gap between them. Instead he brushed a lock of hair away from her face.

"There," he said with satisfaction. "I didn't want it to get in your eye. See you later." He turned and walked away.

Shocked, Isabel stared at him for several seconds before walking back inside her apartment.

Nothing made sense anymore. He'd offered her precisely what she had wanted, but now it turned out it wasn't what she wanted at all.

Determined to make herself relax, Isabel soaked in the tub for over an hour. Her fingertips had wrinkled to a prunish state by the time she stepped out and dried herself off.

Tonight she wanted to look special. She'd be meeting firefighters from another station for the first time and she wanted to make a good impression. She scrutinized every outfit she owned, trying to find the right thing to wear. She wanted to look feminine, but not frail or weak.

It took her forty-five minutes to come to a decision. Wearing a royal-blue jumpsuit made out of spun polyester knit, she stood before the mirror. The draped neckline added an elegant touch but wasn't so fancy that she'd feel out of place in a casual setting.

The sash belt accentuated her narrow waistline, while the straight legs emphasized her statuesque figure.

Allowing her hair to fall free in soft waves around her shoulders, she brushed one side away from her face and pinned it in place with a cloisonné barrette. As she turned to get her purse, the doorbell rang.

Opening the door, she invited Mark inside the apartment. "I'm almost ready. I just want to switch purses."

"Take your time." His eyes appraised her in a quick up-and-down motion. "Nice outfit," he commented offhandedly.

His tone was so flat it bothered her. "Thanks—I think."

He gave her a quizzical look. "What's on your mind?"

"Your lack of enthusiasm. I feel as appealing as a lady who can swat flies with her ears!"

He laughed. "Sensitive, aren't we?"

She shook her head. "Just stating the facts, sir."

"I told you, I'm going to keep everything casual between us. It just wouldn't do to have me tell you that you look so sexy I'm tempted to strip you right here and carry you off into the bedroom."

She choked. Coughing, she glared accusingly at him. "Not much for the middle road, are you?"

He graced her with an accommodating smile. "We aim to please."

She stared at him, then sighed with resignation. "That'll teach me to keep my mouth shut."

As they left her apartment and walked downstairs, she tried surreptitiously to study the man beside her. Black suited his looks well. The coarse cotton shirt accentuated his broad chest, giving only a fleeting glimpse of the powerful torso it concealed. With a tan field jacket thrown over his shoulder, he looked strong, handsome and confident.

There was a vitality about Mark, an eagerness to experience everything at its fullest, that made him the most exciting man she'd ever met. She had a feeling he held nothing back from life. Or from her, should she decide to give herself to him. . . .

She glanced back at him and noticed he was watching her closely. Smiling to mask her thoughts, she spoke quickly. "Tell me about this friend of yours."

His blue eyes caressed her with the warmth of their glow. "Which friend?"

"Of course. I forgot. You have more than one," she teased, trying to break the tension between them. "The lieutenant who's having the party, silly."

"Sam Blake?" He shrugged. "He's a down-to-earth type. That's the reason we get along so well. We're not as close, though, not since he got married."

She picked up the regret in his tone. "Why?"

He gave her a fleeting, weary smile. "He's had to spend a lot of time with his new family. With a two-month-old baby and a wife to look after, he doesn't have much time to go out with the boys."

Look after. The words echoed in her mind.

He gave her a knowing glance. "Now, don't go getting on your high horse. It's normal for a man to want to take care of his family."

"*Be* with his family, don't you mean?" she countered acerbically.

"No. In Sam's case it's 'take care of.' His wife had a very hard pregnancy. Ever since she gave birth, she hasn't been able to get around much. From what I understand, she's had surgery several times since. She'll be all right, according to Sam, but she has to take it real easy for the next few months. They can't afford a nurse for Ann, one for the baby and a housekeeper, so Sam's been taking care of almost everything."

Isabel gulped. "I'm sorry. I misunderstood."

He nodded. "I know." He helped her into his car. As he slipped behind the driver's seat and put the car in gear, he turned to look at her. "I'll give you something else to think about." He paused. "He's had troubles, but I think he's a very lucky man. Annie adores him, and he's crazy about her. If I was in his shoes, I'd be more than happy to do the same thing."

She glanced at him quickly.

"Does it surprise you that much?" He gave her an ironic look. "Be sure you see me as I am, rather than the person you're so afraid I'll turn out to be."

She started to protest.

He held up a hand. "How did we get on this topic anyway?" He gave her a disarming smile. "Let's concentrate on having fun tonight, and nothing else. Is that a deal?"

Relieved, she smiled. "Deal!"

"Oh, I hope you don't mind"—he glanced at her then back to the road—"but I've promised to pick up another friend of mine who lives on the way."

"No, I don't mind at all." She felt as if a great weight had been taken off her shoulders. With another guy along, she'd be distracted enough to keep from dwelling on the situation between herself and Mark.

He made a turn and drove down a plush residential street. The houses, with their steeply pitched roofs and half-timbered facades, looked extraordinarily beautiful. Yards were meticulously sculptured. In the lavender twilight the rose bushes seemed to dance as their brightly petaled flowers swayed in the breeze. Mark slowed the vehicle as they approached a particularly attractive home.

Turning the corner, he pulled into a circular driveway. He parked by the entrance, then turned to her. "I'll be right back."

She nodded, her eyes staying on him as he walked to the front door.

Seconds after he rang, a tall young blond woman appeared. Her slender hips and long legs were encased by possibly the tightest pair of corduroy jeans Isabel had ever seen. Her face lit up the minute she saw Mark. Without hesitation she threw her arms around him. As Mark spun her around in midair in a very enthusiastic hug, her long blond locks trailed inches from her body, weaving a soft curtain around them.

Isabel swallowed. The girl had the qualities of a fashion model. Instinctively she looked down at herself, making a silent comparison.

Leaving his arm around the girl's slender waist, Mark led her to the car. Instead of going to the passenger's side, however, he walked around the car and opened his own door. The girl peered inside.

Too stunned to do anything, Isabel gave her a halfhearted smile. "Hello."

The next instant, the girl slipped across the seat, forcing Isabel to squash herself against the door. "Hi! I'm Sunny!"

Wondering if that was her religion, her state of mind or perhaps—horror of horrors—her name, Isabel continued to smile with the same fixed expression she suspected a dental patient wore before the novocaine lost its effect.

"What's your name?" Sunny asked brightly.

Isabel gritted her teeth. "I'm Isabel Dailey, a fire-fighter at Mark's substation."

"Oh, how exciting!" Sunny graced her with a bright smile; then, as Mark slipped behind the wheel, she grasped his arm tightly and squeezed. "I'm Mark's best buddy."

Isabel tried to act natural, but her stomach felt tied in knots. "I'm glad. Mark needs all the friends he can get." She closed her eyes and cursed herself. *Was she actually jealous? Her? No way!*

"I'm looking forward to this evening," the girl cooed. "I love parties, don't you, Isabel?"

"Just adore them." She tried to keep the sarcasm out of her tone. She didn't really have anything against this girl. She just wished she were somewhere else—maybe Saturn.

"I've got really good news, Mark."

Isabel's attention was riveted on their companion. What did Mark see in her?

"I'm going to get that scholarship I was hoping for!"

"That's great!" His face exploded into an enormous grin.

Isabel looked at the girl. "What scholarship is that?"

"To State. I'm starting my sophomore year at college this fall."

Isabel glanced at Mark quickly. What could he possibly have in common with a girl whose topics of conversation no doubt revolved around classes, clothes and health foods?

By the time they arrived at the party, Isabel longed to escape from the car. Sam Blake greeted them at the door. To Isabel's chagrin, he seemed to know Sunny more than just casually. Had Mark actually *dated* her?

Feeling miserable, yet telling herself over and over again that Mark was perfectly free to see whomever he chose, Isabel tried to act as if the entire matter no longer merited her attention.

Standing in one corner of the room, she listened to bits and pieces of conversations floating in the air around her. A little voice inside her told her she should at least try to socialize, but she dismissed the thought. There was a certain perverse pleasure to be derived from feeling sorry for herself.

She was staring at Sunny, who was busy charming a bevy of firefighters congregated around her, when a deep masculine voice startled her back to reality.

"Can I get you something to drink?"

She turned to look at him. Sam Blake's dark brown eyes were trained on her. He regarded her with a mixture of amusement and benevolence.

She smiled. "Yes."

He smiled back. "What would you like?" He led her to the bar.

Isabel stared at the selection of bottles before her, then glanced at his glass. "Whatever you're having."

"Are you sure?" He gave her a wary look. "I'm having a whiskey sour."

She looked at Mark as he casually draped his arm around Sunny's shoulder. "Make it a double."

With a shrug, Sam prepared it for her. "Most women don't like the taste of whiskey. I'm glad to see you appreciate the finer things in life."

She nodded absently as he handed her the glass.

She wasn't a drinker. In fact she hated the taste of alcohol, but tonight seemed a good time to start schooling her palate. "Thank you."

She took a sip. It was awful. No, she concluded, it was worse than awful. Deciding that perhaps, like medicine, this was best downed quickly, she finished the contents and set the glass down.

Seconds later, she was surprised to find Sam Blake placing another in her hand. Wishing she had never heard of whiskey sours, she gave him a polite smile. "Thanks, Sam."

"There's plenty, but unless you're used to them, I suggest you drink them a bit more slowly."

She met his eyes. "I can handle it. Don't you worry about me."

She took a large gulp. It was really awful. Not wanting to dwell on it, she chugged the rest of the glass. She hated Sunny, she hated Mark, but most of all she hated the taste of whiskey. This time she held on to the glass.

Sam Blake moved off, circulating among the crowd. Another firefighter approached. She recognized his face. He had attended the Academy at the same time she had. "Hello, Joey."

"Hiya, Isabel." He studied the vast selection of liquor spread before him on the bar. At length he glanced up and looked at her empty glass. "What are you drinking?"

"Whiskey sour." Had he been nicer to her during her months at the Academy, she might have felt more inclined to warn him about the taste. As it was, however, she felt herself to be under absolutely no obligation.

"Here."

Turning her head, she looked at him. He was holding out another glass of the light amber liquid. Cursing herself, she gave him a casual look. "Go ahead. I'll fix my own."

"I hate whiskey. I poured it for you."

Hoping by this time her taste buds had committed suicide, she smiled and accepted the glass. She supposed that holding her nose while she drank would really blow her sophisticated image, so she swallowed the drink in several quick gulps, then moved as far from the bar area as possible, still clutching her glass.

Two firefighters who had been talking to Mark earlier approached her. "You must be Isabel."

"Sure." She nodded, and to her horror realized she was beginning to slur her words.

They exchanged glances. "You came with Mark, didn't you?"

"Yep," she replied good-naturedly, then giggled. "But I'm not his date."

"You're not?" the tall blond asked.

"Nope." She gestured with a toss of her head in Sunny's direction. "I'm just along for the ride."

"You mean you think . . ." Once again they exchanged glances.

The dark-haired man, who looked as if he had stepped out of the pages of Greek mythology, laughed. "Well, Sunny's a beautiful lady, all right, but—"

She giggled, interrupting him earnestly. "Isn't it amazing how someone with eyebrows like Groucho Marx can be considered sexy?"

The men looked at her, then began laughing. The tall blond gave his friend a devilish grin. "Sunny's been rated a perfect 'ten' by some of our guys."

"Yes," Isabel gave him a knowing smile, "but that was on her I.Q. test."

The men roared. Hearing their laughter, Mark approached them. "What's going on, guys?"

"We're just talking to your friend," the tall blond answered, then directed his gaze to her empty glass.

Mark looked at it in surprise. "What are you drinking, Isabel?" His tone was guarded.

"Wisskey showers." She smiled, and tried to figure out why she could no longer feel her lips.

With a knowing grin, Mark took the glass from her hands. "It's getting late. I think it's time for me to take you home."

"What about her?" She looked directly at Sunny, who was busy charming several men around her. "She doesn't look like she'sh ready to call it a sh-night."

He laughed as he turned to look at the fair-haired girl. "She'll let me know, then. If there's one thing that can be said for Sunny, it's that she's got a mind of her own."

Isabel giggled. "And she doesn't seem to object to going through life without ever using it!"

Mark looked at her, then at his two friends. Suddenly he began to laugh. "Pete," he asked the light-haired fireman, "would you mind giving Sunny a lift home? I wouldn't trust any of the other guys here."

"No problem, Mark." He stood casually, a beer in hand. "I'm just waiting for my wife now." As a lady in her mid-thirties approached, he smiled. "Here she comes."

Mark greeted the woman. "Hello, Midge. I hope you don't mind, but I asked Pete to give Sunny a ride home."

She smiled. "She lives less than a block from us, Mark. It's no problem at all. Besides, you know how much we both like her."

"Good, then it's all set." He walked across the room, exchanged a few quick words with Sunny, then returned to Isabel's side. "Let's go."

She took a few shaky steps. "I think I'll just stand here."

"No, I'm taking you home now." He lowered his voice to a conspiratorial growl. "Just lean on me. I'd carry you out, but it wouldn't look too good to the guys, you know?"

"I don't need to be carried, Lieutenant!" she replied stiffly.

"Fine." With a wave to Sam Blake, he led her unobstrusively to the door. As they reached the street, he clamped his arm around her waist.

"You don't have to hold me as if I were about to fall, Mark." She concentrated on each syllable, determined to stop slurring the words.

"How do you feel?" As they arrived at his car, he released his hold on her. Keeping one hand on her shoulder, he opened the door.

She slipped inside. "I'm perfectly all right."

He looked at her for a second, then shook his head. With a grin, he added, "That's what they all say."

The world had stopped reeling, but her face felt as if it had been anesthetized. She wished Sam had been drinking ginger ale.

Mark slipped behind the driver's seat. As they got under way, he placed his arm over her shoulders and tried to get her to lean against him.

"I don't want you *now*," she said stubbornly. "Where were you all through the party?" She didn't wait for an answer. "You were so preoccupied with your other 'friend' you forgot all about me."

"I could never do that," he replied quietly.

"Oh, stop it!" She pursed her lips, wishing she could feel them. How long did whiskey take to wear off? she wondered sullenly. "Just don't patronize me, all right?"

"Fine." The corners of his mouth twitched.

She seethed as she debated whether or not to confront him. Finally her self-control faded, and her anger came exploding to the surface. "Just what the hell were you trying to prove tonight? You asked me out on a date, then bring another woman along."

"Date?" He shook his head. "I told you, we'd

continue to see each other, but only as friends." He eased through the city streets, keeping his eyes on the road.

"You asked me out," she countered.

"As a friend." As he neared their neighborhood, he slowed down. Parking in front of her building, he turned to look at her. Suddenly he began to laugh.

Isabel stared uncomprehendingly at him. Muttering an oath, she started to open her door. "I'll see myself inside."

He grabbed her arm and pulled her back. "You're jealous."

"You're out of your mind."

"Admit it, Isabel."

She pursed her lips tightly. "I hate you."

He shook his head. "No. You're angry because you're jealous. I just wanted you to come face to face with that fact."

She looked at him quizzically.

"You can't stake a claim on me unless you're willing to make a commitment."

The thought chilled her. She wanted to cry, she wanted to hit him, she wanted to melt into his arms. "I have no claim on you, Mark. You're free to see whomever you choose."

"Okay." He leaned back against the seat and watched her.

She started to get out, then stopped. "No, dammit! I don't want you to see anyone else."

He smiled. "I know."

Then she hit him. Doubling up her fist, she sent it directly into his middle.

7

Isabel heard the clock radio click on. Seconds later the loud blast of a rock station shattered her eardrums. Jackknifing to a sitting position, she dived toward the nightstand and shut it off. The sound still reverberated in her head.

Closing her eyes, she slid back between the covers. She wanted to die. Her head was pounding ferociously, and her mouth was infernally dry. Her stomach, what there was left of it, felt as if she had swallowed an entire package of cotton balls. Lying between the covers, she wondered if it was time to make out her last will and testament.

A knock sounded at her door. She heard it, but she couldn't move. It sounded again. With enormous determination she stood and walked to the door. "Who is it?" she asked weakly.

"It's me." Mark's voice was unmistakable.

"Go away," she whispered. "Show a little respect for the dead."

"If you don't open this door, I'm going to bang on it so loudly your entire head's going to explode."

She cringed. "All right," she whispered back. "I'm going to unlock it. Then, after you count to eight thousand, come in."

She turned the lock and had begun to amble back across the living room when he walked in.

With a startled gasp Isabel ran to the bedroom and closed the door. She heard his steps as he came toward the door. "Hey, are you in there?"

"No. Go home," she replied morosely.

"You need help?" He was right outside her door.

"Call the rescue squad," she muttered.

He chuckled. "Shall I come in?"

"Do and I'll throw the lamp at you."

His laughter was deep and throaty. "I have something to say to you, when you come out."

"What?"

"I'll tell you when we're face to face."

"Mark?"

"Yes?"

"I hate you."

Isabel dragged herself to the shower. The cold spray hitting her face jolted her awake. By the time she emerged, she was willing to concede that perhaps she wouldn't die after all. However, she told herself grimly, the key word was "perhaps." Putting a robe on, she walked to the kitchen.

"She lives!" Mark's face broke out in a wide grin.

"Keep it up, and you die," she mumbled.

Slumping down on the chair by the kitchen table, Isabel stared at the cup of coffee Mark had poured for her.

His eyes shone with merriment. "By the way," he began, walking to the door, "you left in such a huff last night you never gave me a chance to tell you."

She turned around slowly, afraid that the slightest movement would cause her head to slip off her shoulders and fall onto the floor. "Tell me what?"

He opened her front door. "Sunny's my cousin," he said, quickly ducking out.

Isabel's eyes stayed on the closed door for several seconds, allowing the thought to seep through her consciousness. *She was going to kill Mark the next time she saw him, provided she lived past this morning.*

Forty-five minutes later, dressed in blue jeans and a faded plaid flannel shirt, Isabel walked out of her apartment. Balancing her box of oil paints and brushes in one hand and her canvas and easel in the other, she ambled to her car. Her headache had definitely improved, and with it her general outlook. She was busy placing everything on the backseat when she felt a hand on her shoulder.

She turned. "Mark!" Even in a worn gray oxford shirt and faded brown twill slacks, he looked disgustingly good.

"Hi there, beautiful!"

"After what you put me through last night, I'm surprised you have the nerve to face me." She made a great show of rearranging her equipment and materials inside the automobile.

"Oh, come on," he chided good-naturedly. "If we're going to be friends, the least we can do is occasionally show a sense of humor, don't you think?"

"Your 'sense of humor' escapes me." She stood and slammed the door shut.

"If you're this upset, then I must have been right in assuming you care for me much more than you're willing to admit." He grasped her shoulders and held her steady as his eyes bored through her.

He had a point—one she hadn't particularly wanted to hear, but a good one nonetheless. She took a deep breath. "I'm not angry with you, Mark. I'm simply in a rush. If I budget my time carefully, I'll be able to spend most of the morning working on a painting I've been wanting to do for my bedroom. I just don't have time to stand around and chat right now."

Not giving her a chance to protest, he walked around the car, opened the door and slipped into the passenger's seat. "Okay. I'll go with you in that case."

She strode around the car to his side and threw open the door. "No, you won't. I want a quiet day of relaxation. I want to get away, do a few sketches and some painting. I most definitely do not want to spend today trying to keep you amused."

"I'm willing to admit I made your evening a difficult one last night," Mark said with a grin. "So, with that in mind, I'd like to spend the next twenty-four hours making it up to you."

"Good. Then go home."

"I'm going to be at your beck and call all day," he said, disregarding her statement. "I'll be right there to carry the easel, paints, art supplies, and," he added after a moment's pause, "you too, if you'd like."

"Mark!" She rolled her eyes. "All I want you to do is get out of my car. I won't be able to paint in peace if you're along."

"Do I distract you that much?" He raised one eyebrow in a quizzical gesture.

"Yes . . . uh, I mean sometimes." She closed her eyes, then opened them again. "Mark, let me explain. I like to be alone when I paint, so you're only going to

111

be in the way. Besides, you'll be bored just sitting there and watching me. I won't even be able to keep up a conversation, since I have to concentrate on my work.''

"I don't mind. I just want to share today with my new buddy. I might even be able to help. Besides carrying your gear, I could also be your model. I could pose in the nude.''

"You're not trying to make up for last night," Isabel groaned. "You're trying to drive me crazy today. Right?" She held up her hand. "No, don't answer that." She sighed. "If you insist on coming along, then I warn you I intend to make use of your offer to be at my beck and call.''

"Now you're talking!" He slammed the door shut. "What are you waiting for? We'd better get going if you want to make the most of the daylight hours.''

Isabel tried to gather her thoughts as she drove out of the city. Was he really trying to make it up to her, or was he hoping to somehow influence her into making an admission she wasn't ready for? She glanced furtively at him. Why did he have to be so difficult, not to mention unpredictable? Well, it didn't matter. If she wanted to discourage this type of behavior, then she had only one alternative open. She'd have to teach him a lesson. One that he wouldn't be likely to forget for a very long time. As she formulated her plan, she began to smile.

"Glad I insisted on coming with you after all?" He tilted his head.

"Yes, Mark. It's definitely going to be fun having you along.''

He hesitated briefly. "I'm not sure I liked the tone of your voice when you said that.''

She gave him her most disarming smile. "Actually

I'm rather lucky that you're here. It's a real backbreaker to try to carry all the equipment to the spot I had in mind. Also, it's been a long time since I've had the chance to work with a model. It'll be a pleasant change of pace for me. I'm looking forward to it."

"You really want me to pose nude?" His voice rose slightly, mirroring his surprise.

She considered the idea, then discarded it as too dangerous for her peace of mind. "No, not totally." She shrugged. "Maybe we'll just unbutton your shirt, roll up your sleeves, and position you so that the stream and rocks form the background."

"What stream?"

"Oh, I didn't tell you where we're going?"

He shook his head, his eyes suddenly wary.

"It's in the San Juan Mountains. We'll have to hike through a canyon, then up the hillside. It's a hard climb, but it's sure worth it. There's an old mill up there by the side of the creek. A few feet from it is one of the prettiest cascades you can imagine. It's just the type of scene I've been looking for."

"How did you find it?"

"Luck." She laughed. "I saw it on the jacket of a book I checked out of the library. It looked like such a beautiful place, I decided to try to find out exactly where it was. I asked the librarian and she managed to track down the location for me. I hiked up there a few months ago, and it was even more picturesque than the photograph. It's one of those places that you could never really capture on film."

"But you can on canvas?"

She brushed the hair from her face. "I'm certainly going to try."

"And exactly how do you plan to fit me into the picture?"

"We'll have you stretch out by the edge of the water, resting. You'll be a turn-of-the-century cowboy, taking a break."

"The idea appeals to me," he replied, then added, "particularly the thought that this is going to go in your bedroom. I have this vision of you looking wistfully at it every evening before you go to sleep, fantasizing about me."

She grimaced. "Now, there's a sobering thought." She shifted in her seat. "Since I'm not big on nightmares, maybe I should consider hanging it in a more appropriate place—like the bathroom."

"Ouch! You're not much on building my ego, are you?"

"Lieutenant, the one thing I know you'll never suffer from is delusions of humility." Her smile took the sting out of her words.

"You never cease to amaze me," he replied softly, glancing at the equipment strewn over her backseat.

Her eyebrows furrowed. "What do you mean?"

"I can understand the part of you that wants to be a fireman, but I find it almost impossible to combine that with the artistic side of you."

"Why? The guys all have their hobbies. It's nothing unusual to want to spend leisure time doing something that's completely different from firefighting."

"Yes, but the outside interests the guys normally pick are much more basic. For instance, Artie's into lifting weights. Frank, on the other hand, enjoys gardening. Dennis likes working his two horses. A lot of the other guys are into construction work, but no one I know does anything as refined as oil painting."

"While I'm at the station, I'm expected to work and get along with the men. I find it easier to do that by projecting a certain image. When I'm on my own time, however, I like to give the other side of me I normally keep hidden a chance to come out for a breather. It helps me maintain a balance, if you know what I mean. Underneath my uniform, I'm still a woman. My nature is different, and so are my tastes. If my choice of leisure activities reflects that, it's to be expected."

"It's as if you have two separate personalities," he replied thoughtfully. "During work hours, you're one hundred percent the professional firefighter and you try your hardest to make everyone forget your sex. Yet the woman in you is at war with that part of your life, and demands equal time."

"I wouldn't say 'at war,' really. It's just a matter of not neglecting who I am. You see, firefighting—important as it is to me—is what I *do*. Being an artist and a woman are all part of who I *am*. One cannot supersede the other."

He nodded slowly. "Yes, I can understand that."

"What about you? Firefighting is what you do, but what about the man behind the uniform? What's he really like?"

"I like camping out," he replied. "I like almost anything that keeps me outside. I think if I had a desk job of some kind, I'd go out of my mind. You know what my idea of a perfect weekend is?" He didn't wait for her answer. "Backpacking with some fishing gear and living off the land. It's a challenge to take care of yourself. I'd like to take you with me sometime. I think you'd find it interesting."

"I've never been much on camping out. I like nice clean ceramic tubs, hot and cold running water and food that's truly dead before I have to cook it."

"It looks like I'm going to have to work on your spirit of adventure."

She pulled off the highway onto a dusty road and drove up a narrow canyon. "I'm going to have to park the car here. I might as well warn you, though. The climb might get a little rough, particularly with all my gear."

"Don't give it a thought. I'll take care of carrying everything." He grinned. "For today, you're the boss."

Turning the ignition off, she glanced at him. "Be that as it may," she smiled, "I think you'd better let me give you a hand with my things. I don't think you realize how awkward it can be to carry some of that equipment. I'd been planning to make two trips, so by carrying half the load you'll still be saving me time and effort."

"Trust me. I can handle everything you have in the back."

She pursed her lips in silent contemplation as she remembered the jagged hillside and the rock-strewn passage en route to the mill. "It isn't far, but I don't think you realize what you're getting into." Although she wanted to teach him a lesson, she certainly didn't want to see him end up in traction.

He left the car. "I can take care of it. Don't worry about me."

She watched him for several seconds, then stepped forward and helped him adjust his load. "Are you sure?"

"Lead the way."

She ventured ahead at a slow but steady pace. The canyon, littered with boulders of assorted sizes, and thick with scratchy scrub oak, provided no easy access to the secluded spot she sought. Occasionally she looked behind to verify that Mark was indeed keeping up with the pace she had set. Noting the beads of perspiration forming on his forehead with almost perverse satisfaction, she continued the climb.

Twenty minutes later, they arrived at a clearing. The abandoned mill now lay in a state of disrepair, yet the scene that unfolded before them seemed imbued with a certain fairy-tale quality.

Nestled in a large crevice of crumbling granite, the rough-hewn structure seemed to be tottering on the edge of the mountainside. It had probably stood there, resisting the slow but relentless forces of time, for the last century. From the few curled shingles clinging to the steeply pitched roof, to the iron spikes of the ancient water wheel, the mill remained a final legacy of the mining boom that had once brought thousands of men and women to these slopes.

"I remember the first time I saw this place. It felt as if I had stepped back in time."

"It's a tough journey, but I can see why a painter would be interested in it," Mark replied, trying to even out his breathing.

She struggled to hide her smile. "You ought to keep yourself in better shape, Lieutenant," she teased.

"I *am* in good shape." He set her things on the ground. "Forced marches take a toll on anyone, you know."

"You were the one who insisted on carrying everything." She paused, then added, "Not to mention coming along."

He looked up quickly and smiled sheepishly. "So who's complaining?"

Selecting the vantage point she wanted, she began to set up her easel and paints. "You're still going to model for me, aren't you?"

He bowed slightly. "Your wish is my command."

"How nice!" She smiled mischievously. She took a few steps forward, then stopped. "Let's see," she said pensively. "I think we'll have you lie down on your side here by the edge of the stream."

He followed her instructions. "Like this?"

"Not quite." She crouched down before him. "I'm

going to position you the way I want you, so remember not to move after I'm done, all right?"

"Sure."

"Okay. First of all, take your shirt off and lean back against that log."

There was a tiny hint of a grin as he followed her instructions. Reclining, he gave her a questioning look. "Now what?"

She walked back a few paces, then made a great show of studying his position. After a few seconds she walked toward him. Kneeling, she began to unbuckle his belt. As her fingers fumbled with the catch of his jeans, he placed his hand over hers. "Can I help you with something?"

"No," she replied in a crisp, businesslike tone. "Just stay still and let me arrange you the way I have in mind."

"Yes, ma'am," he teased.

Isabel worked his jeans downward until they rode low on his hips. Although she hadn't actually exposed anything, she could see that the gambit had worked. She'd made him nervous and more than a little self-conscious by touching him intimately, yet remaining professionally aloof.

Pretending to adjust his position, she ran her fingers down the length of his frame. Situating him against the log, she pulled his hips slightly forward in a difficult but undeniably seductive pose—one that would place the very part of his body he was struggling to control under her scrutiny, making it that more difficult for him.

She stood, walked a few steps away, then returned to his side. "Your lower half isn't right." She touched his inner thigh, delighting in the way his muscles quivered beneath her touch. Bending his leg at the knee, she ran her hand dangerously close to the taut bulge that betrayed him, and pulled his outstretched limb slightly forward.

"Isabel . . ." Mark's tone was sensual and rasping, betraying his aroused state.

"Don't move," she commanded, once again adjusting the belt line of his pants. Feeling herself respond to the enticing force his masculinity exerted over her senses, she backed away quickly. "Stay that way while I paint. Any movement can throw my work off. Okay?"

"Isabel, wait." His voice was throaty and low.

"Don't talk. I have to concentrate."

The morning passed slowly. Isabel allowed Mark few breaks, ignoring his complaints of a stiff back. Every time he shifted, she would return to his side and readjust his position, taking special pleasure in the effects her touch had on him.

It was almost four hours later when she finally moved away from her canvas. "Except for a few finishing touches, I think it's basically the way I wanted it."

He groaned. "I've got to move, Isabel. I think my body's going to break in two."

She laughed. "Don't blame me. You said you wanted to model." She offered him a hand up. "Be thankful I didn't take you up on your offer to pose nude."

He stood and rubbed his back. His eyes stayed on her face for a few seconds; then slowly he moved toward her, stopping only inches away. "If I'd been nude while you were running your hand over me, I couldn't have been held responsible for my actions."

She swallowed. Without touching her at all, he easily exerted his dominion over the woman in her. She squared her shoulders in a gesture of defiance. "I spent a very uncomfortable evening yesterday because of you. If I've had a little fun at your expense today, then it's no more than you deserve." She took a halting step backward.

His lips curled into an arrogant smile. "You played a little game this afternoon, but it's backfired," Mark drawled softly. "I know that you want me as much as I want you right now."

"I have no idea what you're talking about," Isabel said in a haughty, imperious way.

He cupped her face in his hands, then brought his lips down over hers. His lips moved in a provocative rhythm.

She parted her mouth slightly, instinctively offering him more. As she did, she felt him tremble with a need as powerful as her own.

Reluctantly he released her and moved away. "I want you, but I won't take you until you give yourself to me freely. It's that important to me, Isabel. But there's something I want to point out to you. Your reaction to me just goes to prove what I tried to make you face last night. You care for me as much as I do for you."

She opened her mouth, but no words came.

He smiled tenderly. "Now, let's see that painting of yours."

She inhaled sharply. "No, not until it's all finished." She blocked his way.

"You said all it needed was a few finishing touches."

"And right after that's done, you can look at it."

His eyes narrowed slightly. "Something's going on. I can feel it." Lifting her up easily, he moved her aside and walked to the easel. His eyes widened and he muttered a curse.

Isabel suddenly began to laugh. "What's the matter? Don't you like it?" Joining him, she stood by his side studying the caricature she'd done. His features, though distorted, held that unmistakable similarity that marked that type of cartoon figure.

"My nose isn't *that* long and I most certainly don't have beady eyes like that!"

"It's all in the perspective," she teased.

"And is that a pistol in my pocket?" He faced her.

She pretended to study the area in question. "Hmmm. Maybe that's just wishful thinking."

"What?" he growled.

Isabel giggled and backed away a few paces. "You heard me."

"I think it's time *I* taught *you* a lesson." He lunged toward her, but she dodged, running away.

Without hesitation, he gave chase. Isabel eluded him easily at first, but after a while her reaction time began to slow down. It was then he tackled her. Breaking their fall with his shoulder, he pinned her beneath him on the grass.

"Say you're sorry for making me go through hell today."

She tried to twist free, but to no avail. "Not unless you apologize for what you put me through last night."

"Why should I?" he goaded with a roguish grin. "You're in no position to bargain."

"You have something there," she conceded. "So what happens if I refuse to yield to your demands?"

"Then I'll just have to kiss you into submission."

His words made her pulse leap. Her lips parted slightly of their own volition.

His eyes held an unmistakable tenderness as he lowered his head, their breaths mingling for an instant before their mouths joined. Not willing to linger there, he feathered tiny kisses over her face, then nuzzled the pulse point in her neck. She gave a throaty cry as she tried to resist the white heat of his passion.

"Unless you give up soon," he breathed next to her ear, "I'm going to forget my offer to be strictly friends."

She struggled desperately for some measure of sanity. She couldn't give in. Fighting the primitive passions that blazed inside her, she pushed him away. "No, Mark. We made a deal," she said slowly, regret evident in her tone.

He stood, then helped her up. "I think we'd better go back."

"Yes, you're right." She led the way back to the spot where she had been painting. "The great outdoors, it seems, is becoming hazardous to our mental health."

By the time they returned to the car, Isabel was exhausted. Considering Mark had insisted on carrying everything back to the car, she scarcely had any reason to be tired. Nonetheless, it had been a trying afternoon. It seemed impossible to want anyone as much as she wanted Mark. It had taken every shred of her resolve not to give in to him. Perhaps it was better not to dwell on this any longer, she concluded.

"Isabel?"

She glanced at him, then started the engine.

"In spite of everything, I had fun with you today."

She laughed. "Come to think of it, I did too, Mark."

Sticking to trivialities, they kept their banter light and casual all the way back to the city. Although she refrained from satisfying her curiosity, Isabel noted how he kept checking the time. Finally, as they approached Brighton, she decided to pry.

"For the past twenty minutes you've been glancing at your watch. Did you have an appointment you just remembered or something?"

He shook his head. "I thought that if we got back early enough I'd give Artie a call. He's going bowling tonight, but maybe I can trade him a late lunch in exchange for his help on a little repair job. I need an extra pair of hands."

"I don't believe it." Isabel glared at him. "Why do you automatically assume that if it's a repair job, a woman is unable to get the work done? That's first-class chauvinism if I ever heard it. Honestly, Mark, that is really insulting."

"I didn't say you couldn't get it done. I just thought you wouldn't be interested."

"Why don't you offer me lunch instead? I'd be willing to help you out. Like the old saying goes, 'Sometimes the best man for a job is a woman.'"

He started to protest, but then with an air of resignation leaned back against the seat. "Just remember that I didn't force this on you."

"Look, you wanted us to be friends. Friends help each other out. If you need something done, I want to be there for you."

"Whatever you say."

They arrived at her apartment twenty minutes later. Mark helped her unload her paints and equipment while she gingerly carried the canvas upstairs to dry.

Storing her materials inside her closet, she propped the painting against the wall, making sure it wouldn't be bumped. "Now, pretend I'm Artie, and let's get to that lunch you offered."

He shrugged. "We'll go over to my place. I'll make us a couple of corned-beef sandwiches and bring out a cold beer."

She grimaced automatically, then smiled. "I'll take the sandwich, but I'll pass on the beer, all right?"

"You don't like the taste?"

"No, and after the way I felt this morning, I've decided to become a teetotaler."

Mark laughed loudly. "Oh, I see."

"Never let it be said that I don't learn from experience." She walked to the door. "I can sure go for that sandwich, though. I'm starved."

They walked out of her building and began to cross the parking lot.

"You know," Mark ventured, "it might be fun to have you as my buddy. I've never really had a woman I could share this kind of thing with."

"Exactly what needs fixing? I gather it can't be too complicated if you just need an extra pair of hands."

He led the way down the hall to his apartment. "Oh, I know exactly how to do the work. It's just that cleaning the carburetor, then tuning up the car is a really messy job, particularly in my vehicle. Nothing's in an accessible place, if you know what I mean."

She had no idea what he meant, but she was starting to get a funny feeling about the whole thing.

Lunch was over much too soon as far as she was concerned. The more Mark talked about the job, the more she regretted ever having opened her mouth. She didn't mind getting dirty, but electrical shocks and minor burns—injuries Mark claimed to have sustained during his last battle with the mechanical components of his foreign sedan—left her less than eager to tackle the job.

By the time they adjourned to the building's garage, she was looking forward to the task as much as she would have a trip to the dentist. She stared at the car; then, as Mark buried his head inside the engine compartment, she reluctantly stepped forward to help him.

The minutes ticked by with alarming slowness. She'd often seen men work on cars, and she'd concluded it couldn't be too dull a job by their enthusiasm. Her opinion was altering.

Mark interrupted her thoughts with a request.

"While I'm cleaning out the main jet on the carburetor, could you drain the oil and clean the oil screen? It'll save us a lot of time."

"Sure," she agreed, eager to speed up the process. She remembered seeing her father change the oil in the old family car several times when she had been growing up. Her first task wouldn't be any problem at all. Anyone could loosen a nut and place a pan beneath, to catch the oil.

Grabbing an adjustable wrench, she crawled underneath the engine. Mark slid the oil pan toward her, then pointed to the area where she'd be working.

"After the oil drains awhile, loosen the five little nuts around the outside of that plate. It'll come right off with the oil screen. After you take it out, you can clean it off with turpentine," he instructed.

Everything went fine until she loosened the smaller nuts. As she pried off the plate, the little washers fell into the basin of old oil. Grimacing, she fished each of them out of the dark, viscous fluid with her fingers. As she started to remove the screen, more of the thickened liquid ran out, pouring down her outstretched arms and onto her sleeves.

She muttered an oath. "Mark, why didn't you tell me there'd still be oil inside when I removed the plate? It ran all over my arms. I'm up to my elbows in slime!"

He laughed from somewhere behind her. "Sorry. I guess you should have waited a little longer for it to drain. I usually leave it until I finish adjusting the valves. That's really the job I need your help with."

Adjusting the valves was easier, since all she had to do was use the wrench to turn something called the flywheel and read the directions from a manual to Mark, who was under the car doing the actual work.

An hour later they finished. She had a small cut on her hand from a scrape during the spark-plug-changing and enough oil on her to give OPEC a run for their money.

"I've enjoyed spending this afternoon with you, Mark. It's been an experience." She helped him return the tools to the metal box. "But next time, feel free to call Artie."

Seriously considering the value of lapsing into the traditional "helpless-female" routine from time to time, she walked back to her apartment.

8

As the platoon went on day shift four days later, Isabel walked to the bulletin board and checked the work roster.

Artie came up from behind her. "Did you hear the news?"

She gave him a wary look. "What are you talking about?"

"The substation intramurals are coming up in three weeks." He paused. "I'll tell you one thing. If we don't beat the guys at Station Forty-four this year, I think the loo's going to have us doing calisthenics from now until the day we die."

"How come?" She crossed her arms in front of her and leaned against the wall.

"Their lieutenant, Phil Jenkins, got out of the Fire Academy at the same time Mark Grady did. They've had this rivalry going between them for years. It's all in good spirits, but it's there. Grady hates to lose to them more than anything else in the world."

"How has our station done in competition against them in the past?"

Artie shrugged. "I was stationed across town last year, but from what I've heard, our loo lost rather badly, and Jenkins made him eat more than just a good helping of crow."

"What types of events are we going to have?"

As he was about to answer, Dennis peered out a doorway. "Come on, you two. We're about to start our meeting."

Artie led the way down the hall. As they entered the kitchen, Isabel noticed the rest of the platoon had already assembled. Mark stood with one leg propped up on an empty metal chair, balancing several clipboards across his knee. Isabel looked at him, but he never glanced up.

Resting against the counter, she waited.

Mark appraised the firefighters carefully. "Almost everyone here is in lousy physical shape." He stared at Frank Lindsey's expanding waistline. "Some of us are worse off than others."

A ripple of laughter echoed around the room.

Frank smirked, then looked at his shoes.

"Since I have no intention of coming out second best in this year's competition, I might as well warn you in advance. We're going to start a rigorous physical training program."

Isabel noted the silence. Normally, the men would have groaned and grumbled, but something in Mark's tone precluded any complaints.

"For your information, I've also accepted a side bet with Station Forty-four. Since it affects all of us, I think it'll give everyone here an added incentive."

Dennis gave him a wary look. "What kind of side bet?"

"If we lose, we're going to have to wash and wax all the vehicles from their station, as well as provide the beer for their celebration party."

"What?" Joe Gutierrez looked at Mark as if he were nuts.

"You heard me." Mark gave them a smug grin. "So unless you guys really love cleaning trucks, I suggest you work real hard to get yourselves into shape."

"You've got to be kidding, Loo," Artie ventured, shaking his head. "Individual scores count for over half the competition, and let's face it, they've got an ace in the hole."

"What are you talking about?" Mark's voice was guarded.

"Haven't you heard?" Artie ran a hand through his hair. "Their new probie is Allan Talbot."

Mark gave him a quizzical look. "Allan Talbot? Who the heck is Allan Talbot?"

"Don't you remember the All Conference decathlon champion?"

Mark muttered a loud oath. "Are you kidding? Jenkins never said a word, the son . . ." He looked at Isabel, then added with a sheepish grin, ". . . of a gun!"

Everyone laughed. Dennis shook his head slowly. "I guess we might as well get used to the idea of washing their trucks, because our chances of winning are about as likely as half the department quitting to join a ballet troupe."

"Not necessarily," Isabel ventured slowly. "Oh, I admit that they've sprung a ringer on us, but that doesn't mean we should give up before we start."

Mark nodded. "She's right. Dennis, before you

became a paramedic, you were a top-notch pipeman. You're tough to beat on the tower climb."

Dennis nodded slowly. "Even if he is a decathlon champ, he doesn't have the experience. If he turns out to be my competitor, I think I can beat his score."

"And if he's not the man you're up against," Artie ventured, "there's no way any of those guys can match your time in that event. Didn't you set a record last year?"

Dennis smiled. "Yea."

Mark's eyes lit up. "You did? Were you the guy who ran the stairs in just a little over two minutes?"

"Two minutes and seventeen seconds," Dennis said proudly.

"Wait a minute. Are you talking about the same tower we had at the Academy? The one that's seven floors up?"

Dennis nodded and chuckled. "What was your time, Firefighter Daily?"

"I'll give you a hint." Isabel grimaced. "I went up and down those stairs so many times during training, I can tell you there are ninety-six steps."

"I gather you didn't qualify right away," Artie teased.

"I made it in the three minutes they gave us," she responded, "but I have to admit, it took the wind out of my sails. Carrying seventy pounds of hose and nozzle, then hustling up those stairs, is no picnic."

Mark looked at Dennis. "Do you think you can maintain last year's time?"

"Sure." Dennis rolled up his sleeve and affected a strongman pose. "See? The only thing I need now is a big red S."

Loud coughing and gagging sounds echoed around the room.

Mark held up a hand. "Artie, are you still lifting weights?"

He nodded. "I like to keep in shape, Loo."

"Good. You'll represent this station in the hose drag. . . . Joe, Frank"—he glanced at both—"you guys will be with me. We'll have the 'pit-fire' event. The record for that is three minutes. Let's see if we can cut our time to two and a half."

Frank looked at him in surprise. "Loo, we have to drive the truck a hundred yards to the hydrant, hook it up, charge the hose and put out a fire. It's impossible to do that in less than three."

"We'll give it a shot." Mark stared back at them all. "Starting today, we're going to begin working out. We'll jog, lift weights, and exercise when we're not out on a call."

"Wait." Isabel stepped forward. "You haven't assigned me anything yet."

The men exchanged glances. Mark just looked down at his pad. "Isabel, you're going to be the coach."

"What?"

"Calm down." He smiled innocently. "Being the coach is the most important job. You won't be competing, but you'll be in charge of everyone's training."

Her shoulders slumped. "Is that a polite way of saying you don't want me on the team?"

"No, no!" His protest seemed a bit too vehement to be sincere. "It's just that since you've recently gone through the Academy, you're going to be more acquainted with the latest physical-training methods. You'd be the one most likely to be able to keep up with whoever you were training."

Dennis snickered, then turned his back. His shoulders were twitching.

131

Isabel pursed her lips. It was obvious they viewed her as ballast, something that needed to be jettisoned before it dragged them all down. "I'm in better shape than Frank. Wouldn't it make more sense to give me an event and let him do the coaching?"

Mark shook his head. "In the 'pit-fire' event, it's experience that counts. You don't have enough of it. Not yet."

This was getting her nowhere. Too proud to beg them to allow her to be on their team, she shrugged. "You want me to set up training schedules? You've got it. But if that's what I'm to do, I want your guarantee that you'll let me handle it without any interference."

Mark nodded, looking immensely relieved. "You've got it."

"Good."

"I've set up some weights in the apparatus room, guys," Mark continued. "I want to see everyone out there at least twice during shift, working out." Mark glanced at Isabel. "When you get a physical-training program set up, let me know. We'll call another meeting and you can fill us in on the details."

She nodded. An idea was starting to form in her head. If they thought she was going to let them off the hook easily, they were in for one big surprise.

The end of their meeting signaled the beginning of their house chores. As Isabel swept and mopped the kitchen floor, she carefully considered her options. What she needed was a series of general exercises designed to build up everyone's stamina and strength. By midmorning she was ready to present her program to the others.

She was on her way to Mark's office when she met him in the hall. "I was just going to see you."

"I'm here." He smiled. Crossing his arms in front of

his chest, he gave her a speculative look. "Is there something I can help you with?"

"It's the other way around. I wanted to let you know that I've got the details worked out on that fitness program you wanted."

"Good. Get the guys and have them meet us in the kitchen in twenty minutes."

Isabel watched him as he strode down the hall. A hint of a smile touched her features. He was in for quite a surprise. She'd get them all in shape, all right. That is, provided they survived.

As the firemen of the night shift began to trickle into the station, Isabel met her colleagues at the door. Dressed in a jogging suit, she gave them a cheerful smile. "Fellows, we're only going to exercise a little bit today. Don't look so glum."

Frank gave her a cold stare. "I have a feeling you're going to enjoy this, Dailey."

"Of course I am," she replied innocently. "I told you I wanted to do my part."

"I think we've created a monster," Artie grumbled.

Isabel laughed. "We'll jog from here to Jefferson High School, go around the campus, then come back."

Frank's eyes bulged. "Are you out of your mind? That's got to be over three miles."

"We'll be taking it real slow, Frank." She gave him a sweet smile. "Surely you can keep up with me."

"You're coming?" His eyes widened in surprise.

"Certainly."

"If you can make it, so can I," Frank replied resolutely.

"If at any time anyone wants to slow down and walk, go ahead. This is our first day, so I don't want anyone to push too hard."

Frank laughed and Dennis joined in.

"Is that your way of saying that if we lose you," Dennis mocked, "we shouldn't worry?"

"No," she replied with a wide grin. "That's my way of saying that those who can't keep up with me shouldn't feel too bad. After all, there's always tomorrow."

Before they had a chance to say anything else, she began running down the street. The men followed her. After the first mile and a half, she looked around. Artie and Dennis gave her a grin that conveyed their admiration and genuine surprise at her athletic ability. Frank, on the other hand, struggled to maintain the pace she had set. Joe was winded, but looked determined to keep up even if it meant calling for the pulmonary squad by the time they arrived at the station. Mark . . . Well, Mark's face, streaked with sweat, was showing signs of fatigue. The diabolical gleam in his eyes, however, was unmistakable. She chuckled softly, silently acknowledging the truth of the old adage about revenge being sweet.

By the time they reached the station, the men were gasping, trying to recapture their breath. Only Artie and Dennis seemed unperturbed.

"Since this is our first week," Isabel addressed the men, "we won't do any other exercises except jogging. Later, we'll start adding calisthenics and work up until we reach about two hours of daily exercise." She glanced around.

Frank muttered a curse. "If your goal is to kill, why don't you just take a gun and shoot us? It'll be faster and less painful."

"Chin up, Frank. Both of them," Dennis laughed. "It'll do you a world of good."

Artie glanced at the others, then grinned. "For the benefit of the dying among us, I think we should continue to hold these sessions at the end of the shift, rather than before or during."

"I agree," Mark replied. "We won't have to worry about going out on call when we're tired out."

Isabel nodded. "Then it's all set. See you guys tomorrow."

For the next ten days she pressured the men into doing more and more exercises. By keeping up with them, she ensured their cooperation, for not one among them was willing to admit she was in better physical shape than he was.

An entire week had elapsed before the men's stamina began to show signs of improvement. This, she noted silently, also resulted in their dispositions undergoing a change for the better. Today, for instance, as she walked into the kitchen for their morning briefing, the men had met her arrival with cursory nods instead of their previous scowls.

Fixing herself a cup of coffee, she waited for Mark to begin. Their daily ritual was by now as familiar to her as the layout of the fire station.

He looked around. "I have some good news for all of you who've been complaining about our exercise program."

Isabel immediately tensed. Mark had promised she'd get no interference. Had he changed his mind?

His eyes met hers. "It looks like the date for the intramurals has been moved up to suit the new fire chief's schedule. Our competition with Station Forty-four will be held this Saturday morning instead of next week."

"What?" Isabel blurted out before she had a chance to think.

"I bet you're terribly disappointed," Frank mumbled. "You missed your calling, Isabel. You should have been a marine drill instructor."

She made a face at him. "But look at the wonderful things I've done for your body."

"When they bury me, I'm sure everyone will say I was the fittest-looking corpse they'd seen in years," he shot back.

Mark held up a hand. "And for those of you who've been wanting revenge . . ."

All eyes, including Isabel's, focused on him.

"It seems that this year the new fire chief has requested a special event for the probies. The lieutenants from all the stations met downtown yesterday afternoon, and we've devised a wonderful little contest for our newest members." His eyes were filled with devilish merriment as they came to rest on her. "We're calling it the Probie Dunk."

Isabel felt her skin crawl. "What's involved?"

Mark pulled out a chair and straddled it, facing them through the open back. "It's real simple. First you run a hundred yards, then you walk across a four-inch-wide board for twenty feet. Right below it is going to be the biggest mud puddle you've ever seen." Laughter echoed around the room. Mark smiled and continued. "Then you climb up a twenty-five-foot ladder, run fifty feet across a rooftop, pick up a loaf of bread, then go down the ladder and across the board to the starting point. The best part is, you can't squish the bread."

Isabel fell onto an empty chair. "You're kidding."

As the men continued to laugh, she stood and faced Mark. "That's hardly a fair trial. The events you guys signed up for are so much easier."

Frank graced her with a smug grin. "Hey, haven't you been telling us how physically fit you are? Prove it."

"I have. Everything I've asked you guys to do, I've done right alongside you."

"You were the one that was complaining about not competing," Dennis added mischievously.

Joe, who had been silent all along, suddenly stood and faced the others. "I hate to interrupt your fun, fellows, but there's one thing no one's mentioned."

Mark gave him a questioning look. "What's that?"

"How much is this going to count?"

Mark exhaled softly. "I don't know. Station Forty-four's really pushing for this. I have a bad feeling—"

The station's telephone rang. Frank answered it, then gestured for Mark.

As Mark stepped into the radio room, the men began to tease her.

"Come on, Isabel," Artie said. "You're in terrific shape. You can run circles around Frank."

Dennis laughed. "That's not much of a compliment, Art. A turtle could run circles around Frank."

"Stuff it, guys," Frank retorted. "I've still got more stamina than she could ever have."

Isabel cocked her head to one side. "You should have told me that the first time we came back to the station after running three miles. I would have been glad to do calisthenics with you for another hour or so."

Frank's face turned red. "Well, what I meant was, I could build myself up a lot faster than you could."

The corners of her mouth twitched. "I know what you meant."

Joe poured himself a cup of coffee. "You guys still don't see it, do you?" He shook his head. "The most important point here is that—"

At that moment Mark walked back into the room. "Brother, have I got bad news!"

Silence fell. Mark's expression heralded nothing but trouble.

"I just spoke to Captain Taylor downtown. It seems

the chief thinks we don't give our probies enough credit. He said that since their event is the toughest, it should count for the maximum number of points."

Isabel smirked. "Don't look as if it were the end of the world. You guys admitted that I'm in very good physical shape. I can hold my own in any competition."

Dennis nodded. "She's right."

Mark shook his head. "You don't understand."

Joe leaned back in his chair and stretched out his feet before him. "I do."

Mark brushed a lock of hair from his face. "That's what you were trying to tell us a little while ago, wasn't it?"

Joe nodded. He looked at the puzzled faces around him. "Allan Talbot is Station Forty-four's probie."

"The decathlon winner?" Artie's voice rose an octave.

"The one and only," Joe answered.

Isabel felt the blood drain from her face.

9

Isabel stood at the edge of the Fire Academy's practice area, waiting. Just a few feet behind her, Mark kept pacing up and down. In exasperation, she finally spun around and glared at him. "Will you sit someplace? You're driving me crazy!"

He stopped in mid-stride. "Do you realize how close this competition's been all morning? It's up to you now. We're four points behind. If you win your event, that will put us ahead to stay."

"I'll give it everything I've got. More than that, I can't do."

He placed both hands on her shoulders. "I'm sorry. I just hate like hell to lose to Jenkins."

She smiled gently. "We've been working together for the past four days. You've watched my progress and you know I've always improved my previous score. Now it's time for you to trust me."

Mark nodded, then took a step closer.

For an instant Isabel thought he would forget where they were and try to kiss her, but instead he stepped back. "For what it's worth, I was glad to have an excuse to spend so much time with you."

"You helped me a lot." She stared at her feet, not wanting to meet his gaze.

"I'd much rather hear you say how much you enjoyed my company."

She chuckled softly, then met his eyes. "I did. Very much, in fact."

His face lit up, but before he could go on, he was interrupted by the loudspeaker announcing her event. Allan Talbot would be the first to compete.

"I sure hope he trips or falls into the mud," she muttered absently.

Mark glanced at her. "I'll keep my fingers crossed."

They watched as Talbot stood at the starting line, then took off at the sound of the whistle. Like a flash of lightning, he covered the hundred yards in a dozen seconds. As he stepped up on the board that bridged the twenty-foot-wide mud puddle, he teetered and slipped off with a splash.

Isabel cheered. "His feet are too big!" With a triumphant cry, she danced around happily.

"You're right." Mark watched the decathlon winner fall into the mud one more time before crossing the board successfully.

He seemed to be able to run the rest of the course without difficulty, making up for lost seconds with excellent coordination and speed. As he began his return lap, he once again met his match on the narrow beam. Twice he fell into the slithery muck, then climbed back onto the wooden plank. The third time, he was successful, and he streaked to the finish line with his muddy bread in hand.

When his time was written on the judge's chalkboard, Isabel gasped. He had still managed to come through with a very competitive score. Three minutes and fifteen seconds would be tough to beat.

Mark pursed his lips. "I think we're in trouble."

Dennis and Artie approached. Exchanging glances, they looked at her.

"Do you think you can do better?" Artie asked casually.

"I can try."

Dennis poked Artie in the ribs. "What's the matter with you? What she needs right now is a little confidence from us. Isabel's not going to let us down."

Isabel groaned. "Dennis, Artie"—she looked at one, then the other—"go away."

"What did I say?" Dennis muttered as he strolled back to the bleachers near the edge of the field.

Mark jammed his hands into his pockets. "What can I do to help?"

"Tell me what's behind this competition you have with Lieutenant Jenkins."

Mark tossed his head back and laughed. "We went through the Academy together. All through training, we were each other's toughest competitor. Neither one of us, however, was consistently the winner. It got to be a game with us. We studied for the lieutenants' test together, and even competed with each other on the exam." He grinned. "Our scores were one point apart."

"Who won?" she asked curiously.

"He did," Mark admitted grudgingly. "I went to our station, and he was assigned Station Forty-four. The competition between us didn't stop. It just got tougher." He shrugged. "Maybe it's just out of habit, but I hate to lose to the guy."

"I understand you two really rib each other afterward."

He laughed. "That's the best part of being the winner." He paused and added, "And the worst part of being the loser."

Mark glanced up and stopped speaking as Artie came toward them.

"I've got a surprise for you," he told Isabel, then handed her a note.

Her eyebrows furrowed. "What's this?"

"Just the incentive you need to win," Artie shot back good-naturedly, then ran back to the bleachers.

The note had been carefully folded. Opening it, she read the message:

Good luck. Mom and I are rooting for you!
                                                    Dad

Isabel groaned. "Oh, no."

Instantly alert, Mark looked at her. "What's wrong?"

She handed the note to him. "My parents are here."

His face lit up in a wide smile. "Hey, that's great! The old chief's here?" He glanced around. "There he is! He's waving at you." Grasping her shoulders, he turned her in the right direction.

Isabel managed a weak smile as she waved back.

"What's the matter? Aren't you happy to see them?"

Isabel looked at her feet glumly. "I'm happy to see them," she conceded. "I only wish they hadn't come just in time to see their daughter wallow in the mud."

Mark laughed. "So don't fall in."

She turned her head and started to respond, when her name was called over the speaker. The other stations' probies had all finished the event. She was the last to run.

"You better get ready." Mark grinned. "Too bad I can't give you a kiss for luck."

"Please!" She held up a hand. "I haven't had my shots yet."

As she took her place at the starting line, her hands began to perspire. If only she could win. She'd prove to the guys that women did have the agility necessary to excel at the job and that at times they'd even be able to best their male counterparts. This was also her chance to show her dad what she could do. She bit her lower lip. She *had* to win!

When the starting signal came, she was off. Only one thought permeated her consciousness: She *would* win!

She crossed the board without mishap and rushed to the ladder. Missing the first two rungs, she slid downward, regained her balance, then scrambled upward again. By the time she picked up the loaf of bread on the roof and dashed back down, she was certain her time was only seconds away from the leading score. Something ingrained deep in her consciousness urged her past the limits of her endurance. Pressing herself for even more speed, she headed back to the board. She was halfway across when she slipped on a muddy spot left by an earlier runner and fell to her knees. Miraculously, she remained on the wooden plank.

Waving her hands in the air for balance and clutching the cellophane bread wrapper in her teeth, she carefully returned to her standing position. Seconds later, she had traversed the remaining length. By the time she returned to the starting line, she was surprised to feel tears stinging her eyes. Wiping them away before anyone could see, she prepared herself to admit defeat with as much grace and dignity as she could muster.

Mark ran up to her. "You did well."

Breathless, she shook her head. "Not good enough, though. That fall I took cost me."

He fell into step beside her as they left the field and headed toward the sidelines. "Let's just wait and see. I timed you, but my watch isn't official."

"Did I do very badly?" Her voice sounded taut even in her own ears.

"Badly?" He stared at her in surprise. "I think you might have won."

"What?"

As her time was printed on the chalkboard, she gasped. She had made it in exactly three minutes. She had beaten her competitor by fifteen seconds! With a yell she jumped up in the air.

"I think your score is going to put us over the top." Mark waited anxiously. As the final tally for each team was printed, he turned, locked his arms around her middle and spun her around.

Artie, Dennis, Joe and Frank ran up to her. Artie hugged her so tightly she thought her lungs would collapse, but before she had a chance to complain, Dennis grasped her by the waist and lifted her in the air as if she weighed no more than two pounds.

Joe interrupted the chorus of congratulations as he saw Jenkins approach. "Loo, I think you're about to have your moment of victory."

Mark chuckled. "Isabel, remind me to buy you the best hamburger in town!"

"Your generosity overwhelms me," she shot back good-naturedly.

Jenkins stood a few feet in front of them. "Mark, good buddy, it looks like we get to wash all your trucks."

Mark laughed. "Not to mention providing the beer for *our* celebration party."

"Yeah, that too," he conceded with effort.

"Aren't you going to congratulate our probie?"

Jenkins grimaced. Extending his hand toward Isabel, he gave her a long speculative look. "If only you had the same shoe size as 'Big Foot'! The outcome might have been different then."

She smiled. "That's one of the advantages of having a woman probie on your team." She glanced at Mark and smiled.

Feeling a hand on her shoulder, Isabel turned. Face to face with her dad, she gave him a cautious smile. "What did you think?"

"I'm impressed." His deep green eyes shone with pride that was impossible to hide. His hair was almost completely gray now, but he still managed to exude the vitality of a thirty-year-old. Leaning down, he gave her a light kiss on the cheek.

His eyes then strayed over Mark's uniform and insignia. "Lieutenant, your station put on a very fine performance."

Mark beamed. "Sir, coming from someone I've always admired, that's quite a compliment." They shook hands as Mark introduced himself.

With a curious mixture of feelings, Isabel watched them. It felt strange to have the two men that meant the most in her life just inches away from her. As they began talking, she noticed the similarities between them. It was as if they had been cast from the same mold. There was an instant understanding between them. Instead of two strangers who had just met, they were conversing with the ease of reunited friends.

"We'll be having a barbecue at Frank Lindsey's house to celebrate this afternoon. Why don't you come along Chief?"

Isabel saw her dad smile. "I'd love to. It'll give my wife and me a chance to be with our daughter, too. That's really the reason we flew in from Florida."

Isabel stood beside Mark. "Why didn't you tell me you were coming? I could have met you at the airport, then driven you back here to Brighton."

"It was really a spur-of-the-moment thing. Chief Taylor called last night and told us you'd be competing. We thought we'd come in and see how well you did. We decided not to call because we didn't want to make you nervous."

Isabel glanced around. "Where's Mom?"

"I'm right here." The voice came from directly behind her.

Isabel turned around and greeted her mother warmly.

A tiny, almost delicate woman in her early fifties, Jennifer Dailey retained, in a mature form, the beauty that she had always shared with her daughter.

As Mark walked off, engaged in a lively conversation with her dad, Isabel watched them pensively. "I thought if those two ever met, they'd get along. I see I was right."

Her mother gave her a knowing smile. "He's very handsome. Are you serious about him?"

Isabel choked. "Mother! Certainly not, so don't get your hopes up."

Her mother's look told Isabel she hadn't been fooled for an instant. "Whatever you say, dear."

Isabel sighed. Her mother had just used the same tone of voice, if not the same phrase, she usually reserved for her father, every time she had wanted to avoid pressing the issue. Suddenly reminded of her reasons for avoiding Mark, Isabel met her mother's steady gaze. "It doesn't really matter, Mom. Even if I were in love with him, I'd never allow our relationship to get serious."

Jennifer Dailey gave her daughter a quizzical look. "Why not? He seems like such a nice young man."

"You don't understand," Isabel retorted in a monotone.

"Then explain it to me," her mother countered.

The sudden directness from such an unexpected source caused Isabel to look up quickly. "I beg your pardon?"

"I said, explain it to me."

Isabel blinked. How could she be honest with her mom without hurting her feelings? She decided to take the easy way out. "I can't talk about it now. I'll tell you later, when we've got more privacy, all right?" She smiled at the two men as they approached.

"I've asked the lieutenant to have dinner with us, Jennifer," Jake Dailey said. "He's invited us to their station's barbecue lunch, so afterward I thought all four of us could meet at the hotel, relax and get to know each other."

Isabel fought the panic that suddenly gripped her. What was the matter? What difference could it possibly make to her if her father and Mark became friends? To her horror, she realized her father had just said something to her and she hadn't even heard him. "What was that? I'm sorry, I didn't hear you," she apologized nervously.

She heard her mother chuckle.

"I was just saying that you should have told us about Mark. He's exactly the type of young man I was hoping you'd find someday."

"Find? . . . Wh-what?" she stammered.

Jake stared at her. "What's the matter with you, Isabel? Have you gone deaf?"

Mark seemed to be fighting to keep his face expressionless, but the corners of his mouth curled in a slight grin.

Isabel glared at him, then tried to figure out what to say to extract herself gracefully from the situation. No words came. "I . . . uh . . . I . . ."

Jennifer came up and placed her arm around her daughter's shoulder. "Isabel and I are going to do a little shopping, dear. We'll meet you two later at the barbecue."

Jake nodded. "Yes, maybe you *should* talk to her." He looked at Isabel quizzically, then shook his head in a disapproving gesture.

"I can't," Isabel hedged, trying to avoid the meeting her mother had in mind. "I promised Frank I'd help get everything ready for the barbecue today."

Mark took a seat on the empty bleachers. "I wouldn't worry about that, Isabel. Frank'll understand."

"I hate to go back on my word," she said, hoping he'd stop insisting.

"Don't give it another thought. I'll talk to him and tell him you won't be able to make it."

"Thanks." Isabel gave her mother a wan smile. There'd be no escaping it now. Wondering how she'd be able to handle it, she began walking to her car. "Where would you like to go first, Mom?"

"Why don't we go to your apartment? I really didn't want to go shopping. All I'd like to do is have a quiet talk with you."

And that's exactly what she had been trying to avoid, Isabel thought morosely. "All right."

As Isabel made her way through traffic, her mother said nothing. The silence was deafening, but Isabel was determined to let her mother take the lead. Having concluded that the best course of action lay in answering whatever questions her mother asked as honestly as possible, she kept her eyes on the road and prayed that her mother wouldn't be too inquisitive.

"Your dad was very proud of you today at the competition."

The unexpected compliment elicited a wide smile from Isabel. "Thanks for telling me. You know, I never thought he'd ever accept my becoming a firefighter."

Jennifer sighed. "You just don't understand him, Isabel. That's your father's way of being protective."

"No, that's his way of being impossible," Isabel corrected, smiling.

"Your problem is that you're too much like him. That's why you two have such a hard time getting along."

"Maybe." Isabel had no intention of arguing the point, but the fact was, if she had to be like one of her parents, she was glad to have taken after her dad. Feeling guilty because of the way she felt, she avoided looking at her mother.

Minutes later, they arrived. Isabel parked near the entrance, then led the way inside. Uncomfortable with the tension between them, she hoped that the time would pass quickly. There was no way of telling what Mark and her father were discussing, and the possibilities added to her growing nervousness.

Turning down her daughter's offer for something cool to drink, Jennifer Dailey sat on the couch. "Isabel, I think it's time we had a talk."

"About Mark? Mom, there's nothing to talk about." She took a seat on the chair opposite the couch and faced her.

"You're obviously in love with him, Isabel. Give me credit for knowing my own daughter that much. Now, what's the problem?"

"There's no problem. I just don't want to get involved with a man like him."

"Like him?" Jennifer leaned forward. "What's wrong with him?"

"Mom, I don't want to get into this." Isabel stood and walked to the window. Staring outside, she avoided her mother's eyes.

"He seems so nice," her mother ventured slowly. "In fact, from seeing Jake and him together, I'd say he's a lot like your father."

Isabel spun around. "That's exactly the problem!" The minute she uttered the words, she realized her mistake.

"I don't understand. You've always idolized your Dad."

"I really don't want to discuss this."

"Isabel, please." Her mother's tone was soft but insistent.

With a sigh, she returned to her chair. "Mom, I don't want to live the type of life you did. You gave so much of yourself to Dad, you simply became an extension of him. I'm not saying that it wasn't right for you, I'm just saying that I don't want the same thing for myself."

Jennifer looked at her daughter for several seconds. "Tell me how you saw the relationship between your father and me."

"All I know is, you never had a life of your own. I don't want that. I have a career. I want to be my own person first, then share who I am with someone else. With Mark, I'm not sure that the same thing that happened to you wouldn't happen to me."

"Isabel, I've lived my life the way I wanted to. I never wanted a career. I got what I wanted. I wanted to be Jake's wife and I wanted to raise a family. That's exactly what I did."

"But at what cost! You lost part of yourself in the bargain!" Realizing she had practically shouted the words, Isabel immediately softened her tone. "I'm sorry. I'm not passing judgment on you—"

"But that's exactly what you *are* doing." Her mother leaned back and smiled. "The problem is, you don't understand what you're judging." She inhaled deeply. "I wanted a man who would shelter me and protect me. Jake knew that and he tried to meet my needs. Obviously, what you want is different. If Mark is truly like Jake, then he'll make the necessary adjustments. Don't condemn your father for giving me what I wanted."

"You wanted him to run your life?" She sounded aghast.

"Not exactly, I just never wanted the responsibility of making the decisions. I was more than glad to let him take care of things. My life was secure. The point you missed, honey, is that I am happy that way. Your father takes care of me. I'm sure there were many times when it would have been easier for him had we been equal partners, but he never forced me into a role I didn't want." She stood. This time it was she who walked to the window and stared outside. "My only regret is that you've never seen that my life-style is a matter of choice, not force."

"But I saw you make compromise after compromise. I still remember when you wanted a job at the gift shop. Daddy absolutely forbade you to accept it."

Jennifer looked at her daughter, then began to laugh. "Oh, Isabel, how could you have misinterpreted things so badly?" She returned to the sofa. "Let me explain. Your father desperately wanted to get a new car, but our budget had already been strained to the limit. He'd done so much for us that I wanted to get a job and save the money we needed. Your Dad knew how much I hated to work outside our home, and when he found out, he refused to allow it." She looked at Isabel. "Do you understand? He refused because of me, because he knew I'd hate it, not because his ego couldn't take it. Oh, I argued with him. I wanted to do it for him, but he wanted me in the one place he knew I'd be happy—at home."

"Are you saying . . . ?"

Jennifer laughed. "Isabel, like any other married couple, we played our little games; but, honey, I've lived exactly the way I wanted."

"Well, perhaps I've misjudged your relationship with Dad," she conceded, "but Mark's still a threat to me."

"How?"

Isabel sat cross-legged on the wing chair. "It's so hard to explain." She paused. "I find myself really wanting to please him."

Her mother chuckled. "And what's wrong with that?"

"I don't want to start making compromises in order to keep him happy, then wake up one day and find out I've lost all the things I valued most in my life."

Jennifer shook her head. "That will never happen. First, if he loves you, he'll never ask you to give up the very things that make you happy. That's not love, sweetheart."

"But—"

"Isabel, loving doesn't make you weaker. In fact, in some ways it makes you stronger than you ever dreamed possible. If Mark is right for you, he'll know what you need to be happy. When a man's in love with a woman, his goal is to please her, not to take away everything that makes her an individual. There's also something you haven't considered. When you do make compromises, you'll do it because of your love for him. Don't be afraid of giving something of yourself. Giving won't destroy you, Isabel, it will simply help you grow. And if there's a matter you can't yield on, you'll know, and you'll find a way to work it out."

Isabel stared at her mother. "I don't know what to say. I guess I've been wrong about a lot of things. I never thought you were really happy with the way things were."

Jennifer shook her head and smiled. "I have a lot of confidence in you, sweetheart. When you discover what it is you're searching for, then you won't allow anything to stand in your way."

Isabel looked at her mother with undisguised admiration, walked to the couch and gave her a hug. "I'll never be able to thank you enough for this."

"Just be happy, dear. That's all I've ever wanted for you." She gave her daughter a wide smile. "And if Mark's the man you want, grab him quick, and don't let him get away."

"Spoken like a true parent!"

As their eyes met, they both began to laugh.

10

Mark greeted Isabel as she walked through the substation doors. "Hi! I really enjoyed meeting your dad yesterday."

She looked at him and smiled. "I'm glad you two got along. It gave me time to talk to my mother, which I hadn't really done for a long time. I think for the first time I really understand her." Walking to the dormitory, she placed her overnight bag down next to her bunk. "Feels strange to be back on night shift, doesn't it?"

He nodded, his eyes trained on her as he watched her with an intensity that puzzled her.

Unpacking a few of her belongings, she stowed them neatly in her locker, then turned around. Tilting her head in a quizzical gesture, she met his eyes.

Mark took her hand in his, then brought it to his lips, his eyes leaving her face for only a moment. "I wish I could make you see that we can't be friends forever."

The light caress ran down her arm like molten lead. "I've been wrong about a lot of things lately, Mark."

His eyes held her as he sat on the edge of her bed. "Have you made a decision?"

She nodded slowly, her feelings for him shining clearly in her eyes. She needed no words.

His face broke out in an enormous smile.

She laughed. "You know, this isn't the way it's supposed to happen."

He cocked his head quizzically. "What do you mean?"

"In my own mind, when I pictured this moment, my man would scoop me up in his arms and make mad, passionate love to me."

Mark stood, then glanced around the partition furtively. Verifying that no one was about, he gave her a roguish grin, then closed the gap between them. His arms wrapped around her waist as his lips approached hers.

The moment their mouths touched, she felt enveloped in a myriad of familiar sensations. It was all there, as if they had never truly drifted very far from each other—the heat, the need, the loving, all combined, sending a fire coursing through her veins. His tongue probed the outline of her lips, then slid inside, seeking the honeyed depths. She moaned softly as his fingers drifted down her spine, gripping her and pressing her intimately against him.

The instant her lips parted with the soft cry, he plunged deeper. She trembled in his arms, leaning on him for support.

With a frustrated groan he pulled away from her. "If only we were someplace else!" He turned away from her, then stopped.

Her gaze traveled up and down his length, then

settled on the power of his maleness, sheathed only by the dark blue cloth of his uniform.

"Don't look at me that way," Mark said in a voice so raw and husky it sent a tremor through her. "I'm having enough difficulty as it is."

Isabel averted her eyes and smiled. Opening the locker, she stood in front of a small mirror she had hung on the door, and brushed back her hair. Using the reflection of the glass to steal one more look, she laughed as he discovered her subterfuge and blew her a kiss.

"Briefing's in three minutes. Don't be late." His tone was crisp and businesslike. With one last look at her, he smiled and strode out of the dormitory.

By the time she walked to the kitchen, the men had already assembled. Spotting an empty chair next to Artie, she seated herself.

Confirming that everyone was present, Mark began. "First of all, I'd like to announce that our station did very well in the citywide competition. We came in second. Station Fifty-seven beat us by only three points."

A cheer went around the room.

"Needless to say, Station Forty-four didn't do quite as well. I believe they came in fourth in the overall standings."

Another cheer followed.

"Now, to the business at hand." Mark paused. "The State Fire Prevention Bureau is giving a workshop on the handling of hazardous chemicals. The newest firefighter at each station and the officer in charge are slated to attend." He looked at Isabel. "That's you and I."

As the company turned to look at her, she felt her face grow hot. Hating herself for blushing, and wondering what the firefighters would think now, she nodded. "When?"

"Tomorrow morning. I'll work out the details with you later." He smiled. "And would you please stop blushing. You're going to give the guys the wrong idea."

Laughter exploded in the small room.

Hating Mark at the moment, she gave him an icy stare.

Ignoring her disapproving look, he continued to read the work roster for the week. "That's it for now, guys."

As the alarm sounded throughout the station, everyone stopped. Artie ran to the radio room, while the rest of the platoon scrambled to the dormitory. Seconds later, they met in the apparatus room dressed in their turnout gear. Taking her place next to Frank at the back of the pumper, she held on as they criss-crossed through the scant evening traffic.

Isabel waited for the telltale signs of fire, but none appeared. As the pumper stopped in front of a residence, she glanced around curiously. There was no sign of a fire anywhere in the vicinity.

Mark left the cab of the truck, then walked up and down the street. After exchanging a few quick words with one of the residents, he signaled everyone to return to the station.

They drove back at a leisurely pace. As they stowed the equipment in the proper places, there were several discontented grumbles among the men of the company.

Isabel replaced her coat and helmet on the wall hook by the pumper. "Frank, do you think this will start a rash of false alarms?"

He muttered an oath. "I sure hope not."

Before the evening was up, they answered two more bogus calls. By that time the mood of the platoon had darkened considerably. When the third alarm came, the tension was thick in the air. Once again, when they arrived at the scene, they discovered nothing amiss.

As Mark walked up and down the block trying to find a clue to the culprit, Isabel waited beside the truck. A young man she recognized from her talk at the high school came up to her.

While they spoke, Isabel made a few quick notes on the back of her business card. Thanking the boy, she ran up to Mark. "I've got something I think you might be interested in."

Mark scowled. "The only thing I'm even remotely interested in right now is finding whoever's been setting off these false alarms."

Isabel smiled as she fell into step beside him. "Then you're in luck." She handed him her business card.

Mark gave her a look of exasperation. "Isabel, for Pete's sake, why are you giving me your business card? If I need you, I know where you work!"

"Read the back of it, Lieutenant," she said in her best commanding tone.

"What's this?"

"The name and address of the one you're looking for."

He stopped in mid-stride. "You're joking."

"Of course not." She crossed her arms in front of her, then gave him a smug grin. "Sometimes, kind sir, a woman is the best man for the job."

He choked.

Raising one eyebrow in a teasing gesture, she walked back to the truck.

Mark strode to a police squad car that had arrived on the scene. Exchanging a few words with the patrolman inside, he ran back to her. "By the way"—he gave her a sheepish grin—"thanks."

"Did you tell the police officers what a talented firefighter you have under you?" Realizing what she had just said, she shook her head. "I mean, working under . . . I mean—"

Mark laughed and shook his head. "Heck no! I told them I did it all myself. Let's face it. Where would you be without your fearless leader?"

Frank strolled up to them. "What's this about a fearless leader?"

Mark laughed. "I was trying to instill the proper respect in our probie."

"I see." He seemed to mull over the words in his mind. "I've noted a definite lack of respect in her, too. The amount of bowing and scraping she's been doing lately has diminished considerably from the first day she arrived at the station."

Artie joined them. "I just realized, Isabel, you were never properly initiated."

"What?" She gave him a wary look.

The men exchanged glances. Mark's face held a trace of a smile. "Let's go back, guys. We want to be available if a real call comes in." He gave Isabel a mysterious glance. "We can continue this thought back at the station."

By the time they returned, Isabel's curiosity threatened to overwhelm her common sense. Envisioning something along the lines of a fraternity hazing, she slipped quietly into the dormitory and hoped they'd all forget.

An hour later, most of the men had retreated to their bunks. One by one the lights began to switch off, and soon the dormitory was couched in silence. Turning off her overhead lamp, she snuggled deep into the covers.

She had just drifted off to sleep when two powerful hands lifted her out of bed, holding a sheet over her. Laughter followed as she screamed and fought. The next moment, she felt herself being set on a cold, hard surface. A cold spray of water suddenly engulfed her. As the icy water hit her warm body, she squealed.

Laughter echoed as the hands finally released her, and she stepped out of the shower stall dripping wet. Removing the sheet from over her head, she stared at the smiling faces around her.

"Welcome to Engine Company Fifty-five, Firefighter Dailey," Artie said with a chuckle. "It's about time you became one of us."

Her chest almost burst with pride as she heard the words. "One of us," he'd said. Feeling as if she had the world on a string, she began to laugh along with the others. Even Dennis was there, joining in.

When the men began to drift back to the dormitory, Isabel towel-dried herself. Damp, but no longer dripping, she made her way down the hall.

Without warning, Mark stepped out of his room and blocked her way. "Congratulations. You finally made it."

"Isn't it wonderful?" she said with breathless pleasure.

He gave off an exaggerated sigh. "My ego's destroyed. I expected that tone of voice and those words to be reserved for me, after we finish what we do best together."

Isabel looked horrified. "Please! You'll shock my delicate sensibilities."

"That's unlikely. You're a lot tougher than you look." His eyebrows shot up. "I have it on good authority."

"What?" She narrowed her eyes and gave him a skeptical look.

"Your father told me all about you."

"What?" she whispered harshly.

"Go to sleep. I want to get an early start tomorrow. We'll take one of the department cars and drive up to Boulder for the workshop. I'm not sure what they have planned, so just to be on the safe side, bring your turnout gear."

"Don't change the conversation now," she pleaded.

"Sorry, Firefighter Dailey, but we're on city time now. Be ready to go right after the end of the shift. Is that clear?"

She gave him a mirthless smile. "Yes, Lieutenant. However, I don't intend to let you off the hook later, when we're on our own time."

"I tremble with fear, Firefighter Dailey."

Ignoring the grin on his face, she continued down the hall.

Isabel met Mark by the entrance to the station at precisely eight the following morning. "Hi." She studied his lean, muscular frame with undisguised interest. The green doeskin slacks accentuated his length, while the partially open long-sleeved yellow shirt revealed only a hint of his hair-darkened chest. That, however, seemed enough to spark her wildly misbehaving imagination.

"You have that look in your eyes again." Picking up the duffel bag at her feet containing her gear, Mark led the way to a white-and-gold station wagon. The department's car sported the official insignia on the side.

She waited for him to unlock the door on the passenger's side. "What look?"

"The one that says your hormones are functioning."

She laughed as she slipped inside. "I don't think I'll comment on that. It's better, I'm told, to keep them guessing."

Mark lifted their gear into the back of the car, making sure their air bottles would not bump together, then settled behind the wheel. Minutes later they were on their way.

"How long will it take us to get there?" she asked.

"About three hours, if we stop along the way to eat breakfast."

She settled back comfortably in her seat. "Are we on our own time?"

"We don't get paid for going to a workshop, if that's what you mean." He glanced at her, then back to the road.

"I'll take that to mean we're on our own time." She smiled slowly. "Now, tell me what Dad told you."

He laughed. "No."

"Why not?"

"Because I love to see you squirm." He paused. "More than that, I'd love to see you try to get it out of me."

"Pervert," she shot back good-naturedly.

"Jealous?"

"You haven't shown me anything I should be jealous of—so far."

"You know, once we leave the city, there's a long stretch of road between towns. Are you sure you want to continue this conversation?" He paused. "Let me put it another way. How far can you jog?"

She laughed. "Okay. Enough dissembling. What did my father talk to you about?"

"His daughter."

"That I already knew." She looked at the strong masculine hands that gripped the steering wheel. For a brief second she remembered the gentleness they had shown her once.

"You're blushing again," Mark commented. "You shouldn't entertain nasty thoughts. You're much too transparent."

Angry with herself, she closed her eyes and opened them again. "Now, to the topic at hand . . ." She grinned. "What did you and Dad talk about?"

"You really want to know?"

"Of course I want to know." She raised her voice, then lowered it again. "Please."

"Mostly, he told me about you. He said that ever since you were a little girl, you've always followed in his footsteps. He figures that's why you can be so stubborn. But, as he pointed out, you're also capable of giving a great deal of love. The fact that you don't give it easily makes it that much more special."

"He said that?"

"He said a lot of interesting things. He told me not to give up on you, even if you didn't seem interested." Mark looked over at her to see how Isabel was taking it. He added gently, "He said you'd always been very careful about showing your emotions, particularly those that you thought would make you seem weak."

"He's right," Isabel agreed after a long pause. "I wanted to be tough like he was. I was trying too hard to be just like him."

"And now?"

"It turns out I never really knew him like I thought I did."

Mark pulled off the road suddenly. "What the hell is that?" He pointed to a cloud of black smoke billowing in the distance.

"I don't know." She followed his gaze. "I didn't think there were any towns in that direction."

"You want to take a look?"

"Sure. It doesn't look like it's more than just a few miles south of us."

He pulled back onto the road and hurried in the direction of the smoke. "Isabel, there's a state map in the glove compartment. See what's out there, will you?"

After a few minutes she pinpointed the area. "Whatever it is, it isn't large enough to be mentioned on the map."

"If the place is that small, maybe they're going to need help."

"Wait. There's a town there, all right. It's Greenway." She shrugged. "Anyway, I think that's where we're heading." As they passed a road sign, she verified it. "That's the place."

The minute they entered the community, they spotted the fire. A small building, described by a sign as the Greenway Town Hall, was engulfed in smoke. Mark parked by the side of the street, then stepped forward as he spotted a group of ill-equipped firefighters confronting the blaze.

Quickly introducing himself and Isabel, he offered their services.

A lean young man in his early twenties wiped the perspiration from his brow. "Lieutenant, we're from Greenway's volunteer fire department. We thought we were doing all right, except we just found out there's a little boy somewhere in that mess." He gestured toward the building. "The problem is, the temperature is so blasted hot around the exits, we haven't been able to get inside."

"Do you have any booster lines?" Mark asked. "We've got our turnout gear in the back of the station wagon. If you can have a couple of firefighters man a hose, I'll go inside while your men keep a constant spray of water over me to reduce the heat. I should be able to make it through that way."

"We'll give you all the help you want, but you don't understand. One of our men already tried to get inside. There are wooden beams blocking most of the entrance. If we move them or chop our way through, we're just going to bring a lot more of the structure down on us. We also tried to smash open some of the front windows, but every time we did, so much smoke and heat came out, we weren't able to go in."

"Let me take a look, then I'll try to think of something." He gestured for Isabel to follow. His eyes were glued on the building as they suited up. "I want you to stay outside, Isabel. None of these guys have proper training, and their presence, in my opinion, constitutes as much of a hazard as the fire itself."

"Stay outside?" She looked at him in surprise. "Are you crazy? You're going to need me there."

"I want you to stay out of the way."

"Lieutenant, I think you're forgetting I'm a trained firefighter. I'm more than capable of lending the necessary support."

He shook his head. "With our guys back at the station you'd be safe enough. They all know exactly what to do. Here, it's a different story. Those firefighters are just boys, for Pete's sake!"

"Which is precisely the reason I should be with you."

"I mean it, Isabel. You're still a probie. I don't want you to get hurt. Stay out of the way."

As he walked toward the group handling the hoses, she fastened her breathing gear. Ignoring his orders, she took a booster line from one of the firefighters and followed Mark inside the burning building.

The minute they stepped through the doors, a wave of heat and smoke engulfed them, almost forcing them back out. Isabel kept the water over Mark, wondering how much longer they'd be able to stand it.

A large beam, partly in flames, blocked their entry into the hall. Mark tried to find passage around it, but after several seconds pointed back to the door.

Leaving the hose in the hands of another firefighter, Isabel came up from behind him. Placing her hand on Mark's shoulder, she yelled, "I can slip under the beam and check those rooms out."

He shook his head. "No! If it falls, you'd be dead. Go back outside."

"But I can do it."

He grabbed her forearm brusquely and pulled her back outside. "What the hell are you trying to do?"

"Mark . . ."—she lowered her voice—"we're the only two with proper equipment, not to mention training. There's a kid in there—trapped, injured, or hiding in hopes the fire won't find him. We've got to do something."

He nodded. "You're right." He looked down the side of the building. "Let's go take a look at those front windows."

Isabel saw the cloud of dark gray smoke pouring from inside. The first two rooms were engulfed in flames. As they approached the third, she studied the opening.

"Come on," Mark urged. "That's too small to crawl through."

She followed him around the building. The windows on both the north and south sides were much smaller than those facing the front. The back of the town hall was a solid wall of stucco.

"Mark, I think I can get in through the front."

"Using that little office window?" he asked, aghast. "Are you crazy? There's no way you could get inside."

166

"Not with my breathing gear"—she paused—"but I could crawl through, then have you hand it to me."

"No way!" He pursed his lips. "You have no idea what you'd find at the other end. The floor in there could cave in right under you, and there'd be no way to get you out."

"I'll be careful. I won't put my weight on it until I'm sure."

"No, and that's final," he ordered.

She glanced around. Everyone else was still at the front, fighting the fire. "Mark, I don't know what's got into you, but I'm going in there. You know darn well I may be the only chance that kid's got."

There was a pained expression in his eyes as they met hers. Reluctantly he nodded. "I wish I could go instead, but I'm just too big to fit through that opening." He paused. "Just be careful, all right?"

"You bet, boss." She gave him an encouraging smile. "I'll be in and out before you know it."

11

꙳ᦊᦊᦊᦊᦊᦊᦊᦊᦊ

Pressing the flat of her back against the window frame, Isabel slipped her body through the narrow opening. As she swung her legs around, she tested the floor. Satisfied that it was safe, she lowered her weight onto the wooden surface. From behind her, Mark directed a fine spray from the booster line at the ceiling, allowing the water to drip down over her gear, cooling it, making her more comfortable in the hellish environment.

Crawling on her hands and knees through the clear zone only inches above the floor, she avoided much of the intense heat as she searched the room methodically. The child was not there. With slow deliberation she began edging forward out of range of the hose, away from the cooling spray. Her gear began to soak up the heat, making her skin feel dry and prickly. As she moved out to the hall, a dark black cloud extending almost to the floor engulfed her. The smoke stung her eyes. Blinking several times, she began to inch down the corridor, crouching low to remain below the dark, searing haze.

Several of the rooms around her emitted flames that danced and flickered with a life of their own. Her body was drenched with perspiration. The temperature soared as she passed the next two rooms. On her stomach, she continued to move farther into the building, refusing to give up her search. By the time she reached the end of the hall, the temperature had dropped again. As she glanced up, she came face to face with the door to the men's room.

Removing her glove, she touched the door with the back of her hand. It was warm, but no more so than the floor she lay against. Satisfied she wouldn't be greeted by a blast of superheated air the moment she opened it, she turned the knob and crawled inside.

Smoke had not yet claimed this area. Enjoying a respite from the heat, she slowly lifted herself from the floor. Kneeling, she glanced around. It was then she heard someone cough. Immediately she turned toward the sound.

A young boy, about four or five years old, was huddled in the corner. His eyes seemed abnormally large in the paleness of his face. Isabel approached him slowly, hoping her smile would show despite the breathing mask. Talking to him in a voice she knew sounded like it was coming from inside a goldfish bowl, she tried to soothe his fears. She was inches from him when the child reached out and wrapped his chubby arms around her neck. For a brief second she held him, her mind busily gauging the best avenue of escape.

Unable to remove the face mask and risk incapacitating herself, she spoke slowly and carefully. "I want you to play a little game with me, all right?"

The child nodded.

"Have you ever ridden piggyback?"

Again the child nodded.

"Okay." She smiled and unhooked the fasteners to her jacket. "I want you to keep your arms around my neck and lock your legs around my waist." She waited while the boy complied. "Now, I'm going to close you up inside where you're safe, and we're going to pretend I'm a pony and you're riding upside down, all right?"

His solemn little face lighted up briefly.

"Just one more thing." Isabel paused. "I want you to close your eyes tightly and keep them closed until I say so, all right?"

He nodded, his lower lip trembling slightly.

Isabel rehooked the jacket, enclosing the child against her. With his curly black hair visible just below her neck, she edged toward the door. As they worked their way down the hall, he began to cough. Instinctively she increased her speed. The second she entered the room where she had first gained access to the building, she looked up, searching for the window.

Mark's smiling face stared back at her. "What took you so long?"

"I stopped for a soda along the way." Under the cooling water spray once again, she edged her way across the room, unfastened her canvas jacket, and handed the little boy to him.

Mark maneuvered the child through the window, then turned, handing him to a local firefighter. Shifting his attention back to Isabel, he helped her out and back onto the ground.

For a second he stood before her, his eyes shimmering, tempting her with their intoxicating warmth. As they headed back to the pumper, Mark exchanged a few words with the volunteer chief.

When he returned to her side, he was smiling. "They've got everything under control now. Shall we go?"

She didn't really know where he had in mind, but it scarcely mattered, for she wanted a few minutes alone with him more than anything else.

He glanced around; then, as someone took their photograph, he laughed. "Let's get out of here."

"I'm with you," she replied.

Walking briskly, they returned to the car and stowed their gear. Once again, an onlooker took a photograph.

Mark helped her inside, then, diving behind the wheel, made a hasty departure. "I have a feeling we might make their local headlines."

"Does it bother you?" She tossed her firefighting jacket onto the backseat. Slipping the heavy canvas pants off, she readjusted the waistband of her own slacks.

He shrugged. "Not really, but I'd rather have their own department take the credit." With one hand on the wheel, he removed his jacket, tossing it on the backseat next to hers.

She nodded. "So would I."

He handed her his handkerchief. "Boy, are you a mess."

With a grimace, she began to wipe her face clean.

As they left the scene, Mark glanced at his watch. "There's no way we're going to make that workshop in time."

She looked down at herself, then quickly back at him. "Were you still planning to go?"

"Not really." He shook his head and laughed. "There's a gas station just ahead. I'll stop there and call our headquarters. I'll explain what happened and tell them we're going to head back to Brighton."

"Do you think it'll be all right?"

"Oh, sure. There are lots of other firefighters going, so we probably won't even be missed. My bet is they'll just reschedule us and we'll get to go at a later date."

Slowing down, he turned and parked by the gas-station office. Standing by the side of the car, he removed the last of his turnout gear, the heavy-duty canvas pants. "Here. Put these with our other stuff." He handed them to her. "I'll be right back."

By the time he returned, she'd finished wiping the soot from her face and hands. His handkerchief, however, had turned practically black. "I hope you're not especially attached to the color white."

He smiled at the sight. "It wouldn't do me much good if I was, would it?"

As he pulled back onto the road, he reversed directions and began heading south. "I thought we'd unwind by taking the scenic route back. I hope you don't mind," he explained.

"I'm not in any rush." What she wanted was the chance to be alone with him. She looked at him and with a contented sigh settled into her seat.

"What's that all about?" he asked.

"I guess I'm just happy."

He smiled but said nothing. As the minutes passed and his silence was unbroken, she began to suspect there was something wrong. Perhaps the fire had tired him more than she'd thought, Isabel concluded.

She tried to make small talk to help him relax. "A long time ago I used to come to this area to paint. If memory serves me right, there's a very pretty spot not too far from here."

"Oh no, are we in for another forced march?"

She laughed and shook her head. "Not at all, you'll like this spot, I promise. Just turn left at the next dirt road."

He slowed his speed. "What dirt road?"

"Here." She pointed to her left.

He slammed on the brakes. "Nothing like advance notice, I always say." He paused as he glanced ahead. "This isn't a dirt road, Isabel. It's nothing but a trail."

"It'll be all right. Trust me. Keep going."

"Whatever you say."

Fifteen minutes later, they ran out of road. "Now what?"

"We get out and walk." Leaving the car, she ran ahead, then stopped.

His steps were slow and methodical as he joined her.

"Tired?" she asked softly as she led him into a grove of trees.

"A bit, I suppose," he answered casually.

She studied him out of the corner of her eye. The lines around his forehead had deepened. His mind seemed miles away. "Are you angry with me for some reason?"

He looked at her in surprise. "Angry?" He shook his head. "Isabel, that's certainly not what I'd call the emotion I feel for you."

He caught her against him and his mouth descended on hers, taking her breath away, and a wild exhilaration spread through her. His lips parted gently, seeking stronger pleasures, awakening the desire she'd fought so long against. Drinking in the sweetness of the moment, she pressed herself against him, answering the hunger she felt in his kiss with a wild savagery of her own.

Her response fanned the flames of passion he'd

173

held in check, and with a groan he slid his hand downward until he cupped the fullness of her breast in the hollow of his palm. "You're mine, Isabel. Mine!"

She didn't understand the intensity with which he spoke the words, but it hardly mattered. Reality was spinning away. Sensations, both primitive and powerful, held her steady in his arms. Drugged with longing, she clung to him.

Seeking a secluded spot, he led her deeper into the ring of tall pines. Finally, satisfied their privacy would not be disturbed, he lowered himself to the lush grass, then tugged her gently downward.

He undressed her slowly, lingeringly taking his pleasure with each new revelation. Resisting her efforts to unclothe him, he laughed, a deep sensual sound that left her trembling with unabashed desire.

Pushing the straps of her brassiere down, he exposed the fullness of her breasts. His eyes grazed over her with a thoroughness that heated her blood. His rough fingertips sought a honey-brown peak, teasing it into submission with feather-light caresses. His lips sought her eyebrows, her lashes, blazing a trail down her cheekbones. He dragged his tongue across her parted mouth, evading her silent invitation.

Soft little animal sounds escaped her lips as she arched against him, needing him more than she had ever thought possible. She uttered his name over and over again, the urgency that held her captive to his will making her words sound like a soft plea.

He caressed each breast with a forbearance that tempted her sanity; then his hand dropped slowly. Unfastening the zipper of her jeans, he bared her to his gaze.

"My beautiful lady," he murmured in her ear. "How I've wanted to feel your softness, to bury myself in you."

He devoured her nakedness, plundering it with fiery kisses that robbed her of all reason. She clutched at him desperately, her fingers digging into the hardness of his shoulders. His hand slid downward until it reached its goal. Her fists clenched as her hips strained upward against him.

Isabel's mind reeled as his mouth traveled the length of her, his tender caresses turning her liquid, melting her like candy in the summer sun.

It was as if the world was exploding before her, flashing in brilliant, blinding colors. When he released her, she buried her head against him.

He held her until with renewed energy she pulled away. "Now it's my turn to make love to you."

As he lay against the soft blanket of grass, she undressed him. Her hands lingered over the flesh she exposed, enjoying the way his body responded to her touch. His corded muscles tightened beneath her palms as she stroked him. "Don't move. Let me enjoy you as you enjoyed me."

When she had removed all his clothes, she lowered her mouth to his, then settled her upper body over his torso. As she moved sensuously against him, his arms tightened around her waist.

She wriggled free, nuzzling the hollow of his neck, then branding his flesh with moist kisses that caused his fists to clench with a passion that couldn't be concealed.

She ran her palm down the length of him. As she reached the resting place she sought, his lips locked on hers and he pushed her backward onto the velvety grass. Opening herself to him like the petals of a flower, she succumbed to the power of his love. Then they lay still, content for the moment to bask in the warm afterglow.

When she stirred at long last, she found him looking at her. "Hello." She smiled gently.

"You're the most incredible woman I've ever met." Mark's voice was deep, echoing with an intimate timbre.

The breeze that rustled through the pines sent a shiver up her spine. "It's starting to get chilly." She sat up and began to gather her things.

Mark stood and dressed quickly. Holding her hand securely within his, he led her out of the forested area.

As he lapsed into an uncomfortable silence, Isabel began to worry. She was now certain something was troubling him. "Tell me what's wrong?"

"It's something I've got to work out." He shook his head. "Don't worry about it."

"But I am worried. I have a feeling it's something to do with me."

He glanced at her but said nothing.

As they approached the car, he helped her inside, then eased himself behind the wheel.

Before he had a chance to start the ignition, she placed her hand on his forearm. "Wait. I don't want to leave here until we talk this out."

He leaned back against the seat. For several seconds he stared at the road ahead. He seemed to struggle with himself, as if trying to come to a decision. At length he turned and faced her. His palm caressed the side of her face. "I love you."

"I love you too, Mark, more than I ever dreamed was possible. I know now that we belong together." She reached for his hand, then cupped it between both of hers.

Bringing her to him, he held her tightly in his arms for several minutes. His lips brushed her forehead tenderly. "I've wanted so long to hear you say that."

"I'm yours, Mark, as you're mine." She pushed away. "But tell me what's wrong. Share with me what's bothering you. "I'll help. Neither one of us has to shoulder anything alone anymore."

Looking away, he pursed his lips. Seconds later he met her gaze. "If I asked you to give up being a firefighter, what would you say? I'd make it up to you by doing everything in my power to make you happy for the rest of your life."

Her heart constricted. "All you have to do to keep me happy is to give me your love." She paused and added, "And to let me be myself." Isabel felt as if she were being strangled slowly. The bitterness at the back of her throat refused to go away. Her worst fears had suddenly been confirmed. The moment he was assured of her love, he sought to change her by taking away her career. Knowing that he was offering marriage in its stead made her feel worse. Ultimately would she have to choose?

"And if I couldn't accept those terms?" He watched her intently.

"I'd try to explain how much I love my work," she hedged. "You see, there's a danger in asking someone to give up what she loves doing. I might agree, but I don't know how I'd feel about having been forced to make a choice."

"I see," he responded, avoiding her eyes.

"I don't." She gave his hand a gentle squeeze. "Mark, exactly what are you saying?"

"I never thought it would bother me, but today when you went into that building, when I sent you in there, it nearly tore my guts out. My watch told me you were gone only six minutes, but it seemed like hours. I would have given anything to trade places with you, to have protected you by keeping you outside."

"It's all part of the job, Mark."

"I know." He stopped, then continued slowly, considering each word before speaking. "You see, Isabel, I care so much for you that my first instinct was to look out for you, to shield you. But I finally realized I had to let you do what you were trained for, even though I knew you'd be risking your life. It was the hardest decision I've ever had to make."

"But you accepted it. That's all that matters."

"Accepted it?" He shook his head slowly. "Not really. I just know I can't smother you with my love and still expect to keep you." He paused. "It's something I have to come to terms with. I love you enough to let you be yourself, but it's going to be a difficult adjustment. You see, what it comes down to is this: in order to keep you, I have to risk losing you."

"Mark, you've known I was a firefighter all along."

"Yes, but it's one thing to have you work a fire when I'm right there beside you. It's quite another to know that if we marry, they'll send you to another station and you'll be facing dangerous situations without me." His eyes held her in warm study. "You wouldn't be just my girlfriend, Isabel. You'd be my wife, the one woman I'll share the rest of my life with."

"Mark, I don't want to lose you, but please don't ask me to give up the work I love."

He shook his head. "I'd never do that. Firefighting is in your blood as much as it is in mine. To walk away from it would be like giving up a part of yourself." He started the engine. "All I'm asking for is a bit of time to make the adjustment."

But would he be able to? she wondered. And if he couldn't, would she be able to give it all up for him, and not grow to hate him someday for forcing the decision on her? Was she destined to face the choice she had tried so hard to avoid?

He seemed to read her thoughts. "No, Isabel. Without that part of you that wants so desperately to have this career, you wouldn't be the woman I fell in love with. I'm afraid this is out of your hands. I have to decide if I'm strong enough to risk what it takes to keep you."

12

~oooooooooo~

Almost a full week had passed, yet Mark had seldom spoken to her. Sometimes she'd catch him looking at her, a curious mixture of emotions etched on his face. She wanted desperately to reach out to him, to soothe his fears, to love him and have him love her, but she kept her distance. He'd asked for time, and the least she could do was respect his wishes.

It was late morning by the time Isabel finished her groundskeeping duties. Ready for a coffee break, she started toward the kitchen. The sound of loud laughter echoed in the corridor. Voices tinged with admiration joined together in a myriad of congratulatory remarks. The teasing undertone, so common among the fire-fighters whenever praise was well deserved, piqued her curiosity.

As she walked in, Artie grinned, then started what became an enthusiastic round of applause and cheers.

"Who'd have thought she'd turn out to be front-page material!"

Her eyebrows furrowed. "Front-page what?"

Mark gave her a sheepish grin. "The Greenway Fire Department called our headquarters. The chief phoned our station and gave Frank the news when he announced he'd be stopping by today. They're planning to honor us with a special presentation," he muttered, obviously embarrassed by the attention.

Isabel stared at him. "How in the world did they track us down?"

He stood by the head of the kitchen table and opened his hands in a gesture of sheer resignation. "Remember the pictures they took?" He held up a copy of the Brighton *Daily News*. "Our reporter got ambitious."

Isabel stared at her photograph. Her blackened features made it difficult for anyone to identify her, but Mark's scowling face was unmistakable. And so was the insignia on the side of their department's car. "Oh, my!"

Dennis graced her with a lopsided grin. "I guess women can be useful to the department at times."

She laughed and shook her head. "You mean it took you all this time to catch on?"

Artie poked him in the ribs. "Some of us are just a little slower than others." His expression made it easy to see that another crack at Dennis' expense was sure to follow. "Of course, with Dennis, you're talking world record."

Isabel looked up and met Mark's eyes. "What's this about a presentation?"

For the first time since she had known him, Mark turned a deep crimson shade. "It's just a P.R. thing," he mumbled. "It's nothing."

"Some nothing," Frank laughed. "He's getting promoted to captain."

Looking down at the floor, he shrugged. "You're being advanced to firefighter first class, too."

With a triumphant whoop Isabel leaped into the air. "Are you kidding? This is terrific!"

Mark chuckled. "I guess so."

She looked at him. "Don't you want to be captain?"

"Of course I do," he said quietly. "I'm just not much for all this fanfare."

"I am," she said with a lopsided grin.

The men laughed. "That much we can see," Joe commented. Hearing footsteps down the hall, Joe walked to the doorway. "Good afternoon, Chief," he greeted loudly.

The men exchanged glances.

"We better get back to work," Dennis said in his best businesslike tone.

"Right!" Artie followed him out the door.

By the time the chief sat down, the kitchen was empty, save for Mark and Isabel.

"First of all"—the chief looked at Mark, then at her—"I want to tell you how grateful this department is to have people like you."

Mark murmured an embarrassed thank-you. Isabel, stifling an urge to smile, nodded.

"The local media have been calling my office all morning. Everyone wants a chance to interview you both. I've set up a press conference for you later this evening." He cleared his throat. "Of course, you're not obligated, but the department can always use favorable publicity. We'd like very much to get your okay on this."

Mark rubbed his chin with one hand. "I can see where the department might benefit, particularly around budget time, from this type of exposure." He glanced at Isabel, who nodded her assent. "That makes it unanimous. We'll be there."

The chief shook hands with both of them.

"Where will the press conference be held, and what time should we be there?"

"It'll be at seven-thirty in our downtown office," he informed them. "By the way, we're going to announce your promotions and make an official presentation at that time. Effective this evening, you're now Captain Mark Grady." He looked at Isabel. "And you're Firefighter First Class Isabel Dailey."

The exhilaration coursing through her made it difficult to maintain a businesslike facade. Unable to stop smiling, she stood as Mark accompanied the chief back outside.

Eager for time alone with Mark, she waited in the kitchen, hoping he'd return and they'd have a few moments to talk privately. After ten minutes she walked to the radio room. "Hi, Frank. Have you seen the lieutenant?"

"He left. The chief took off, then Grady came back inside and told me he'd be out the rest of the shift."

With a knot at the back of her throat, she nodded. "Fine." She tried to keep her voice steady.

"You don't have to stick around either, if you'd rather not. The shift's over in another twenty minutes and your replacement is already here. I know you probably have some things you want to get done before the conference this evening."

"You heard?"

He nodded. "The chief invited all of us to attend before he left."

"Okay." Her heart felt heavy, but she managed a smile. "I think I will go ahead and leave early. There are a few things I'd like to get done."

By the time she left the station, the nervous excitement that had gripped her earlier had disappeared. In its stead was a dull, oppressive feeling. She felt as if there was an immense weight on her chest.

The drive home did little to lift her spirits. This should have been the best day of her life—she was now a full-fledged firefighter. Instead, her thoughts were only with Mark. Had her promotion precipitated his decision to call an end to their relationship? With her career firmly established, had he decided his future lay with someone else?

The thought made her feel weak and drained of vitality. Losing him was like losing a part of herself, a part she'd never be able to replace.

Alone in her apartment, she tried to divert her mind to other matters. The decision was out of her hands. Why dwell on it? Yet the thought continued to haunt her.

A few times she picked up the telephone, intending to call him, but after dialing the last number, she'd invariably lose her courage and quickly hang up.

Time passed slowly. For want of something to do, she fixed a light snack. Leaving it practically untouched, she walked into the bedroom and began to rummage in her closet for a clean uniform. Functioning despite the burden she carried in her heart, she slipped into it, dropping her soiled one onto the floor.

She stood before the mirror, assessing her appearance. Her freshly polished shoes sparkled even in the muted light of her bedroom. Brushing her copper hair into a loose French knot, she adjusted her cap over it. It was going to be a long, difficult night. With her senses partially numbed from the force of her confused emotions, she left the apartment and walked to her car.

Isabel wanted to resign herself to the real possibility

that she might have lost Mark forever, yet something within her refused to lose hope. Disgusted with herself, she drove to the downtown offices. As she pulled into the parking lot, she saw that several press vehicles had already arrived.

She was just leaving the car when Mark came toward her. "Hello." He was smiling.

She gave him a wary look. "Hello."

"I'm glad you're early too. There's something I want to talk to you about."

She held her breath, praying it would be good news.

As he opened his mouth to speak, the chief waved and called to them.

Mark muttered a soft curse. "I guess it'll have to wait." He looked mysterious.

Isabel fought the urge to grab his arm and order him to say whatever he had to say quickly. "It's important, isn't it?" she asked as she fell in step beside him.

He glanced at her. "Very."

It was impossible to read his expression.

"Today's probably going to be the most important day in your life." He smiled. "Relax and enjoy it."

She looked up quickly. "Wait. Are you talking about the presentation or do you mean—?"

The chief met them at the entrance. Greeting Mark and her warmly, he led them to a large conference room inside. Special tables had been set up at the front. As the chief took his place by a small podium, a hush settled over the crowd of reporters and cameramen.

Isabel saw several familiar faces. Her eyes stopped as she saw Artie make a circle of his thumb and forefinger and flash her an encouraging smile.

When the chief began to speak, she turned her

attention back to her superior. Mark stood and received a small box containing his new gold badge. Immediately afterward, the chief presented her with a small case containing her silver badge signifying her new status and promotion to firefighter first class.

As they returned to their seats, the chief concluded his remarks. Mark removed his badge from the box and pinned it on. Isabel watched him fidget nervously in his seat, then suddenly felt him press the box that had contained his new insignia into her hand. She looked at him in surprise, but before she could ask him to explain, the chief had called on Mark to speak.

Mark glanced around the room. "Gentlemen, we're proud of the job we do," he started.

Isabel fiddled with the container in her hand, wondering what he wanted her to do with it. Absently she pried it open. With a sharp intake of breath she stared at the small diamond ring nestled inside.

"What were you thinking when you consented to have the most inexperienced member of your station go into that burning building alone?" one of the reporters asked Mark.

"It's difficult for any officer to give a new firefighter the liberty of handling a dangerous situation on her own. Still, accepting the fact that all our people are highly qualified professionals, that's precisely what we must do." Mark's eyes met hers. "It all comes down to trusting a professional firefighter to do what she was trained for. With the department, as in life, we can only keep our people by giving them the freedom to pursue their own destinies."

Mark's eyes met hers. Isabel smiled. Glancing down at the box in her lap, she extracted the ring, slipped it onto her finger, then laid her hand on the table for him to see.

Mark smiled gently. "But my decision was really a lot more difficult than you could ever imagine. You see, Firefighter Dailey is going to become my wife."

YOU'LL BE SWEPT AWAY WITH SILHOUETTE DESIRE

$1.75 each

1 □ James	5 □ Baker	8 □ Dee
2 □ Monet	6 □ Mallory	9 □ Simms
3 □ Clay	7 □ St. Claire	10 □ Smith
4 □ Carey		

$1.95 each

11 □ James	29 □ Michelle	47 □ Michelle	65 □ Allison
12 □ Palmer	30 □ Lind	48 □ Powers	66 □ Langtry
13 □ Wallace	31 □ James	49 □ James	67 □ James
14 □ Valley	32 □ Clay	50 □ Palmer	68 □ Browning
15 □ Vernon	33 □ Powers	51 □ Lind	69 □ Carey
16 □ Major	34 □ Milan	52 □ Morgan	70 □ Victor
17 □ Simms	35 □ Major	53 □ Joyce	71 □ Joyce
18 □ Ross	36 □ Summers	54 □ Fulford	72 □ Hart
19 □ James	37 □ James	55 □ James	73 □ St. Clair
20 □ Allison	38 □ Douglass	56 □ Douglass	74 □ Douglass
21 □ Baker	39 □ Monet	57 □ Michelle	75 □ McKenna
22 □ Durant	40 □ Mallory	58 □ Mallory	76 □ Michelle
23 □ Sunshine	41 □ St. Claire	59 □ Powers	77 □ Lowell
24 □ Baxter	42 □ Stewart	60 □ Dennis	78 □ Barber
25 □ James	43 □ Simms	61 □ Simms	79 □ Simms
26 □ Palmer	44 □ West	62 □ Monet	80 □ Palmer
27 □ Conrad	45 □ Clay	63 □ Dee	81 □ Kennedy
28 □ Lovan	46 □ Chance	64 □ Milan	82 □ Clay

YOU'LL BE SWEPT AWAY WITH SILHOUETTE DESIRE

$1.95 each

83 ☐ Chance	97 ☐ James	111 ☐ Browning	125 ☐ Caimi
84 ☐ Powers	98 ☐ Joyce	112 ☐ Nicole	126 ☐ Carey
85 ☐ James	99 ☐ Major	113 ☐ Cresswell	127 ☐ James
86 ☐ Malek	100 ☐ Howard	114 ☐ Ross	128 ☐ Michelle
87 ☐ Michelle	101 ☐ Morgan	115 ☐ James	129 ☐ Bishop
88 ☐ Trevor	102 ☐ Palmer	116 ☐ Joyce	130 ☐ Blair
89 ☐ Ross	103 ☐ James	117 ☐ Powers	131 ☐ Larson
90 ☐ Roszel	104 ☐ Chase	118 ☐ Milan	132 ☐ McCoy
91 ☐ Browning	105 ☐ Blair	119 ☐ John	133 ☐ Monet
92 ☐ Carey	106 ☐ Michelle	120 ☐ Clay	134 ☐ McKenna
93 ☐ Berk	107 ☐ Chance	121 ☐ Browning	135 ☐ Charlton
94 ☐ Robbins	108 ☐ Gladstone	122 ☐ Trent	136 ☐ Martel
95 ☐ Summers	109 ☐ Simms	123 ☐ Paige	137 ☐ Ross
96 ☐ Milan	110 ☐ Palmer	124 ☐ St. George	138 ☐ Chase
